VOLUME
ELEVEN

Sa

SAGA, VOLUME ELEVEN. First printing. November 2023. Published by Image Comics, Inc. Office of publication: PO BOX 14457, Portland, OR 97293. Copyright © 2023 Brian K. Vaughan & Fiona Staples. All rights reserved. Contains material originally published in single magazine form as SAGA #61–66. "SAGA," its logos, and the likenesses of all characters herein are trademarks of Brian K. Vaughan & Fiona Staples, unless otherwise noted. "Image" and the Image Comics logos are registered trademarks of Image Comics, Inc. No part of this publication may be reproduced or transmitted, in any form or by any means (except for short excerpts for journalistic or review purposes), without the express written permission of Brian K. Vaughan, Fiona Staples, or Image Comics, Inc. All names, characters, events, and locales in this publication are entirely fictional. Any resemblance to actual persons (living or dead), events, or places, without satirical intent, is coincidental. Printed in Canada. For international rights, contact: foreignlicensing@imagecomics.com. ISBN 978-1-5343-9913-6

ga™

BRIAN K. VAUGHAN
WRITER

FIONA STAPLES
ARTIST

FONOGRAFIKS
LETTERING + DESIGN

CHAPTER

SIXTY-ONE

Will you marry me?

Are you fucking kidding me?
I've never been more serious, my dearest.
Then where the hell is the *ring*, my dearest?
I, *uh*, haven't had a chance to, you know... to purchase one just yet.
But, I didn't want to leave for the front without letting you know that you're the only woman I will ***ever*** love.
Yeah, you've told me that a thousand times.
Marko, what's this really about?

I'm scared.
I'm scared I won't make it back to you.
Hey, a healthy fear of death is what's going to keep your immaculate ass alive on the battlefield.
I'm not afraid of dying, I'm afraid that, as soon as I finally wet my blade with the blood of one of those winged butchers... I'll never want to quit.
Silly boy.
You just remember how it feels to wet that heavy blade of yours in *me*.
Mmn, is this the part where you entrust me with your grandparents' priceless old *rings*?
You are one dumb young cunt, Gwendolyn.
What?
You thought I loved you?

Nobody even *likes* you.

hhh

Seriously?

You're *sleeping* with him?
Hell.
It's... mighty good to see you, Sophie.
I mean, what about --
My wife and I mutually agreed to spend some time apart.
I was planning to tell you in a more appropriate manner, but apparently, your *dirty laundry* couldn't wait.
Well.
Are you happy?

Do you know what's inside those scrolls?
No, ma'am.
The numbers of every parent on Wreath whose son or daughter was killed in action *last week*.
Do you know how many calls I've had to make?
To those absolute broken husks?
I have some idea.
You ask if I'm happy?
I will be, when I'm never handed one of those goddamn things again.
Look, Soph, you got every right to feel how you do about... this.
But me and Gwen, we're *working* on something, something important.
I thought you didn't care for *"politicking."*

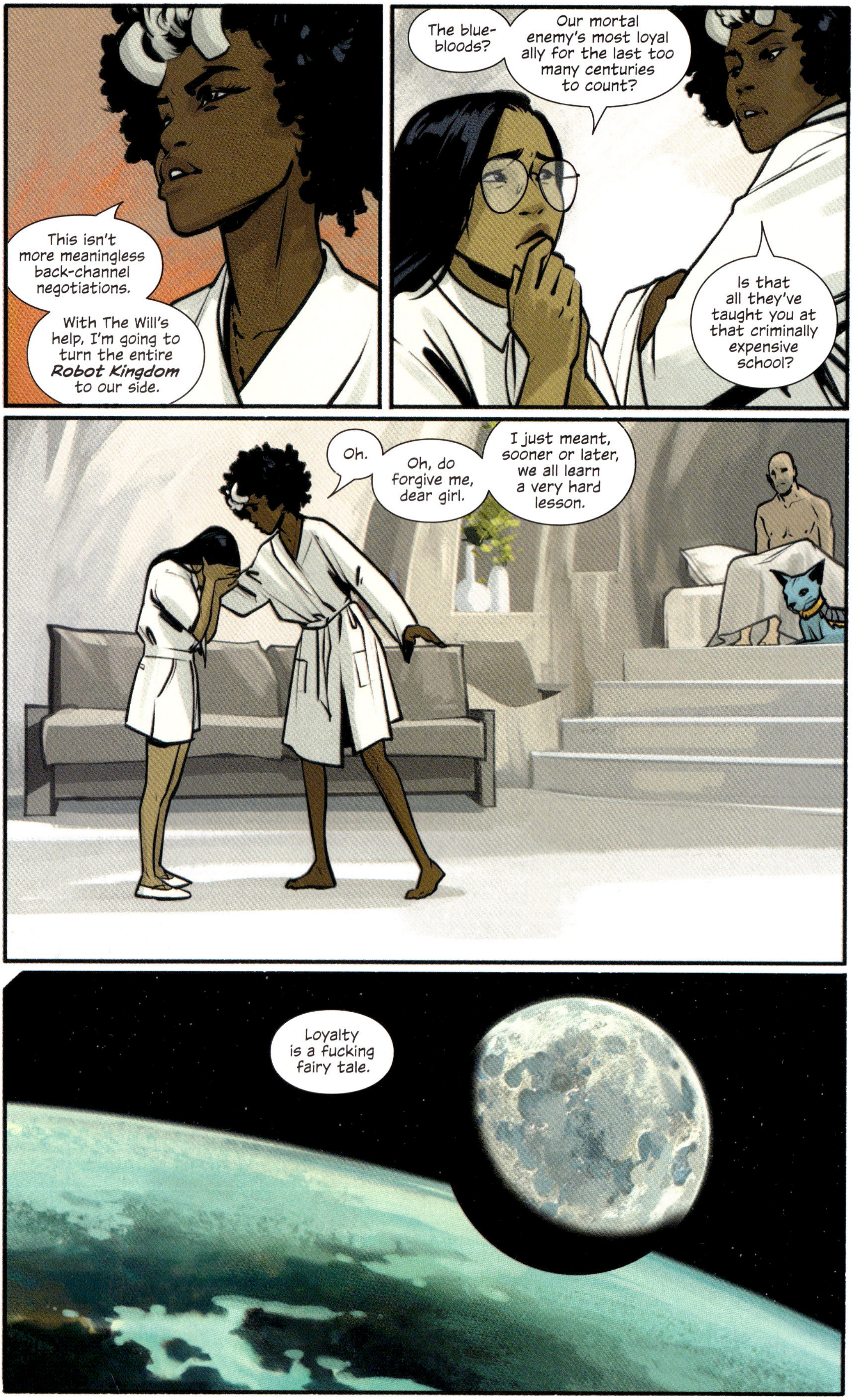
This isn't more meaningless back-channel negotiations.
With The Will's help, I'm going to turn the entire **Robot Kingdom** to our side.
The blue-bloods?
Our mortal enemy's most loyal ally for the last too many centuries to count?
Is that all they've taught you at that criminally expensive school?
Oh.
Oh, do forgive me, dear girl.
I just meant, sooner or later, we all learn a very hard lesson.
Loyalty is a fucking fairy tale.

It had been six months since my family lost our home in a fire.
Inevitably, the world where we were stranded became yet another front in the galaxy's endlessly expanding war.
Lured by its abundant (if haphazardly distributed) resources, a few hundred soldiers from my late father's moon were first to plant their flag.

They were followed by a few thousand troops from Mom's old planet, thrust into an already terrified civilian population.
The rest played out as per usual.
Folks from all sides of this clusterfuck were still chasing after me, but my family and I had never felt safer.

Anything Helps
Suddenly, we were invisible.
I say, you by the squalid tent!
Maybe not to everyone, but like ninety-nine percent of you.

One doesn't often observe commoners this far from the realm.
Has anyone ever told you that you have somewhat... **regal** features?
Yeah, that's 'cause he's secretly a long-lost ***princeling***.
Now can we please have some bread or water so we won't die tonight?
The few who did see us never looked long.
Ah.
I'm afraid my unit is somewhat... defensive of our rations at the moment, but I may have a coin or two for --
Yo, Marquess II!
Less talking, more helping!

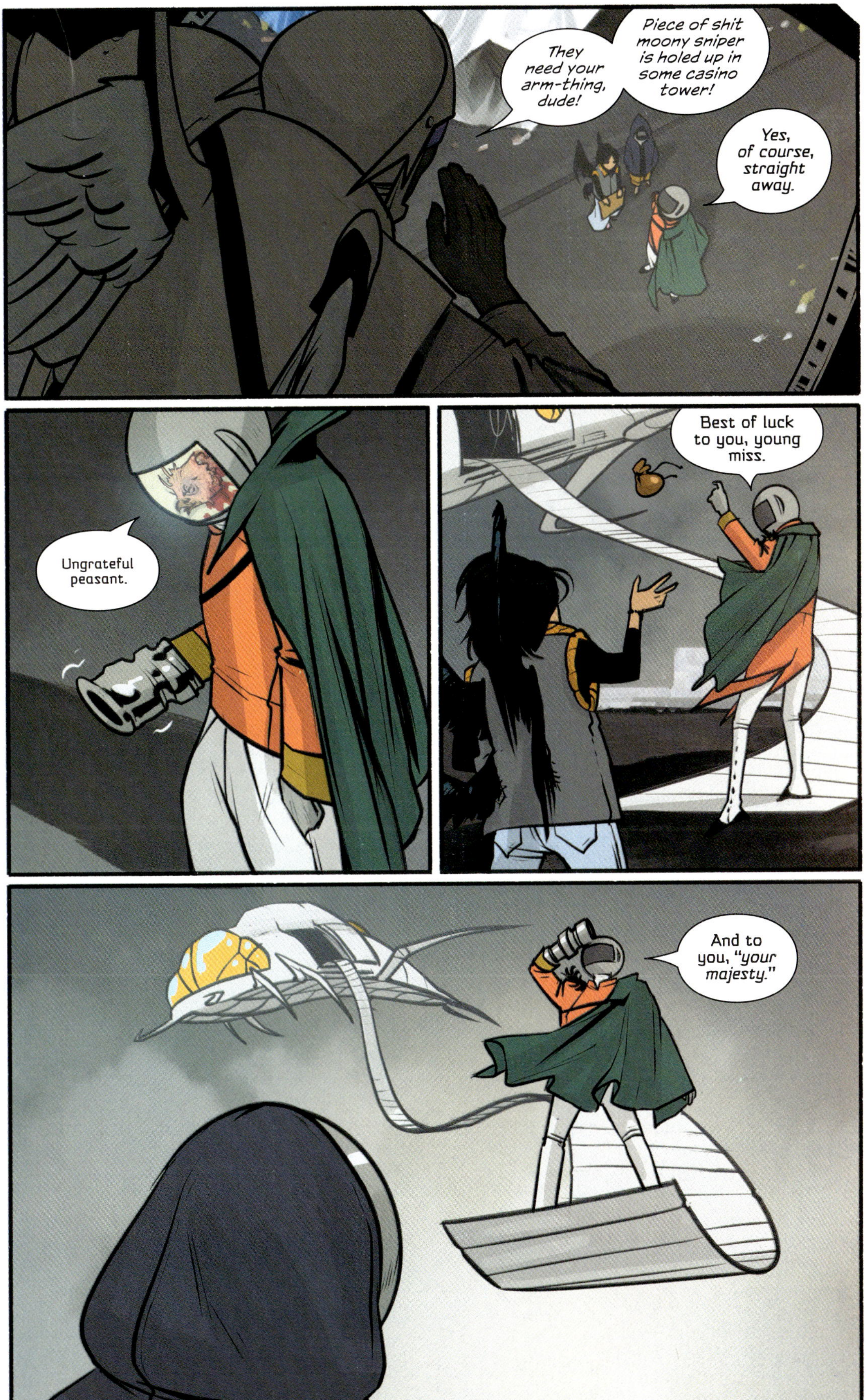
They need your arm-thing, dude!
Piece of shit moony sniper is holed up in some casino tower!
Yes, of course, straight away.
Ungrateful peasant.
Best of luck to you, young miss.
And to you, "your majesty."

Finally.
This thing's starting to give me a rash.
Are you kidding me, kids?
Obviously, not everyone who's "unhoused" (or whatever the correct euphemism is at the moment) is also unemployed.
Hazel, keep that charmer on tight.
And Squire, what's with the aggro shirt? It's just gonna get us more loitering tickets.
Mom had picked up a gig in a nearby warehouse doing something called fulfilling... which was not.

Still, while her meager pay couldn't keep a conventional roof over our heads, Mom somehow kept us alive, which I wish I could say my brother and I always appreciated.
We don't *know* it was the Constables who burned down our rocket.
Yeah, they only openly threatened to, like, a million times.
ACAB
Look, I know every-thing about life is terrible at the moment, but I give you my word that this will *not* be forever.
So until Mama can buy us a little escape velocity, we've got to keep playing it smart, okay? Around the clock?
Thank you.
Now come on, let's run a few errands before Secret Book Club.
Brobot and I made almost five from busking.
Can we eat at Free Refills tonight?
I'm fairly certain that's not the official name of the establishment...
...but sure, let's live a little.

So this nice-looking barkeep -- like a seven, seven and a half -- asks what I do.
I brag how I used to represent some big-time Freelancers like The Button, The Dig, The Skiddoo, and this barkeep interrupts me, she goes, *"Hang on, what's a Freelancer?"*

Can you believe it?! Zero respect for a profession that's probably kept the war off her fucking doorstep too many times to count, am I right?
Hello?
Son?

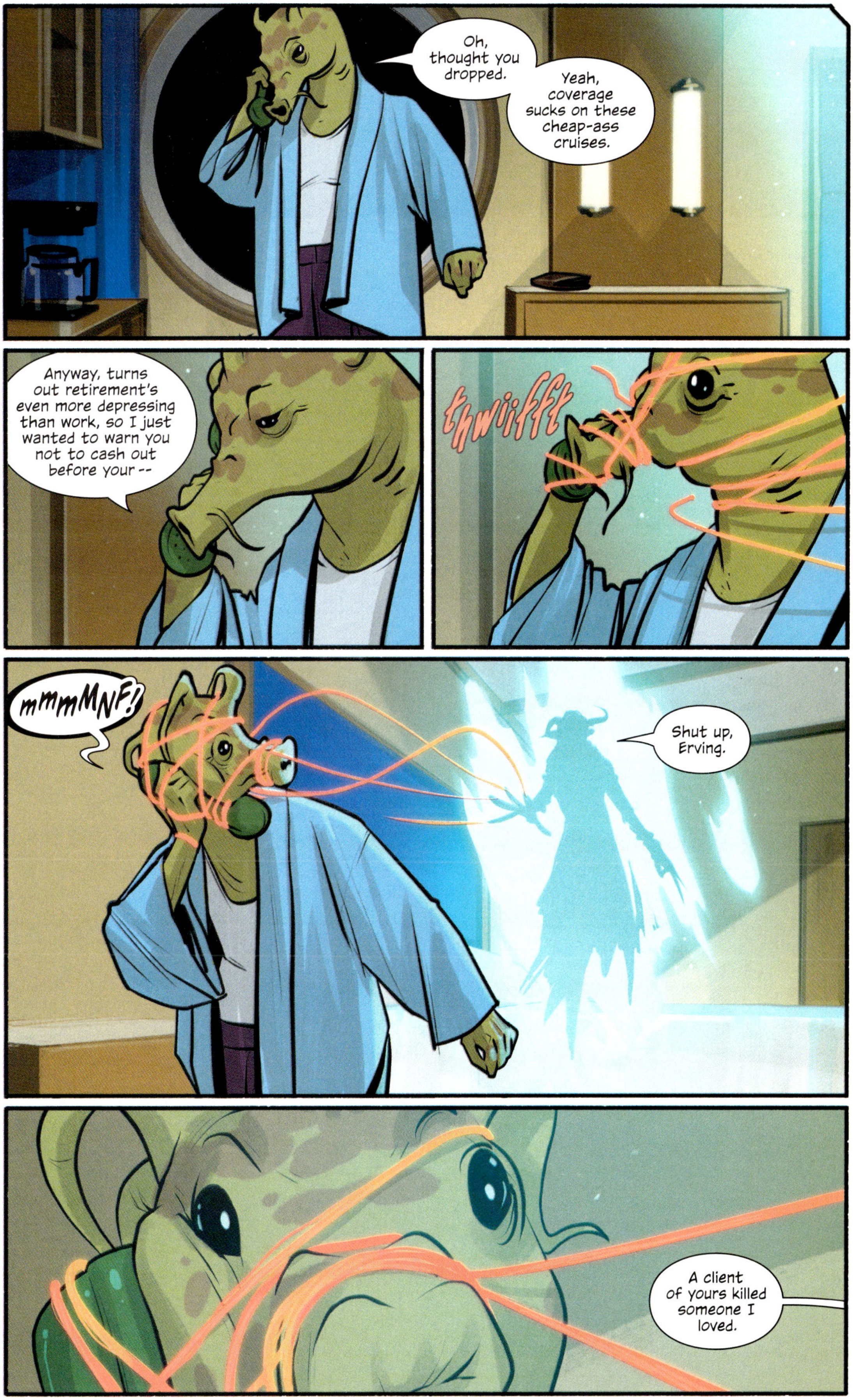
Oh, thought you dropped.
Yeah, coverage sucks on these cheap-ass cruises.
Anyway, turns out retirement's even more depressing than work, so I just wanted to warn you not to cash out before your --
thwiifft
mmmMNF!
Shut up, Erving.
A client of yours killed someone I loved.

Now you're going to help me find The Will.
We hadn't seen my old friend Petrichor since she and Mom had some kind of falling out.

PAWNSHOP, POTIONS & MICROWAVE REPAIR
I didn't get all the details.
No matter how much I wanted to talk about the past, Mom said my head needed to be in the present, my heart in the future.
Remember, no sticky fingers.
Miss Vitch has cameras.
I've got to talk a couple of trades with her, but *if* I have anything left at the end, you may each pick out one small--
Can I please get an enchanted dagger?!
That's not a terrible idea, actually.
My favorite haircut!

I just got a bunch of trashy old paperbacks in a deal, been saving them for you, on the house.
You're a saint, Vitch.
Also, I wanted to talk about something... sensitive.
Another glamour?
I can maybe get my hands on one if you have more medallions to swap.
Worse, I need **paper-work**.
I'm trying to get a job off-world, but the kids and I can't catch a ride without the proper documents, which will be challenging for us to get... conventionally, at least.
Sweetie, do you just need some **forgeries**?
Of course, let's make a deal!

Oh, god, amazing.
Um, I don't know if you accept weapons, but this is a Coalition model Heartbreaker that still --
Pass. They're non-lethal, and they don't even work on drones, no offense to your boy.
Well, what about the last surviving acorn from the entire Rocketship Forest?
And wait a hundred years for it to maybe grow into a healthy vessel?
Please, for all the risk I'm taking, I need something of fair market value...
...like that funky ring that lets me understand you?
No.
No, I'm sorry, but this is all I have left of him.
Wait, you're a widow? Why didn't you say so? You want me to do something about that?
Thanks, but I'm not looking for a love potion.
And I'm not offering one. Girlfriend, I have the still-beating heart of a baby dragon in my freezer. What I'm saying is, we live in a universe of fuckin' magic.
And yeah, the ingredients are expensive, but get me the right ones...

...and I can bring your husband back to life.

end chapter sixty-one

CHAPTER

SIXTY-TWO

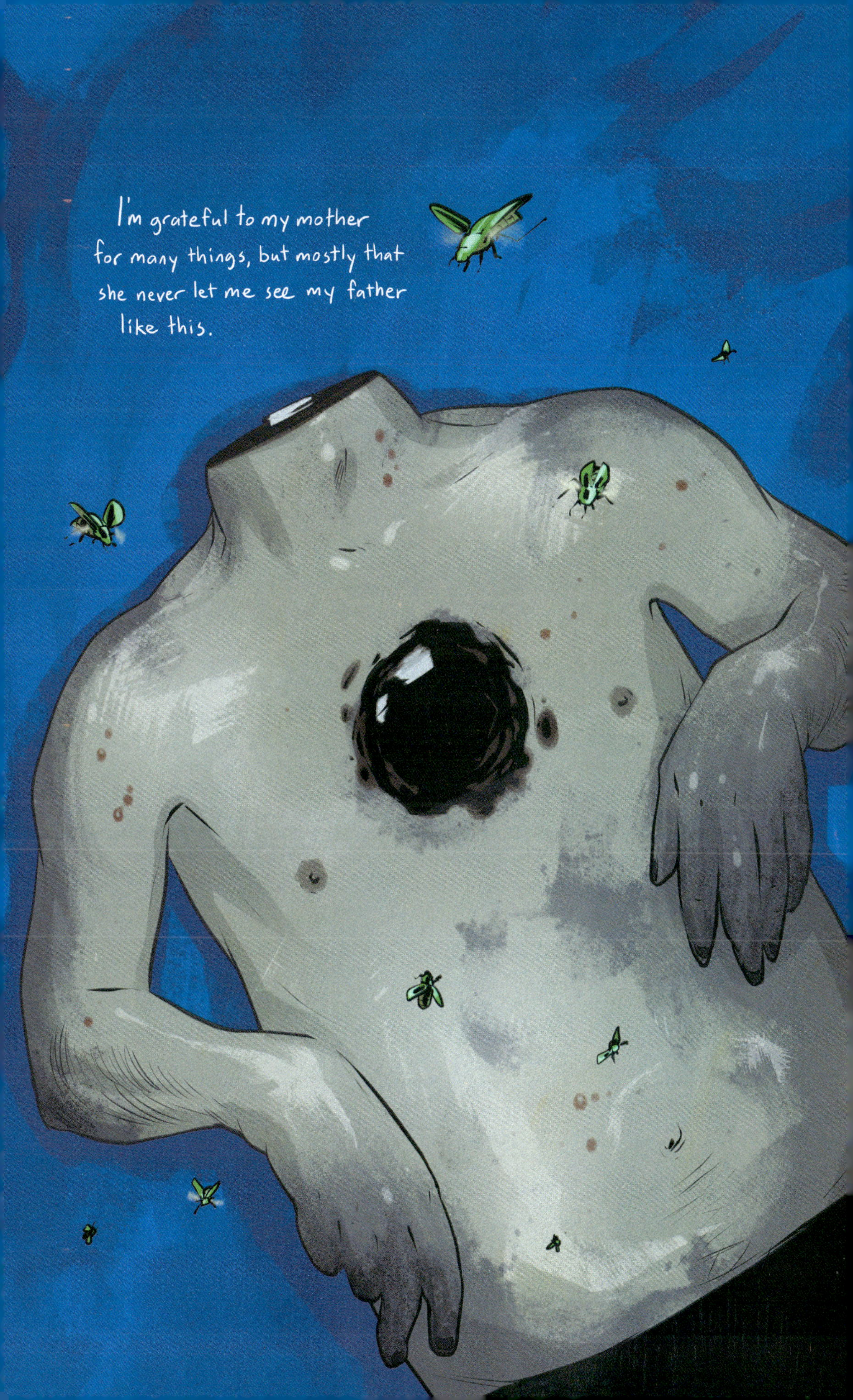
I'm grateful to my mother for many things, but mostly that she never let me see my father like this.

A few years back, a family friend helped Mom track down these remains to a moon not far from where Dad had been murdered.
My deepest condolences. I only wish --
Snow.
Petrichor, what if we could make some snow?
Back on Cleave, Marko once got injured, *mortally* almost, but I... I found the ingredients for a *healing spell*. Couldn't we...?

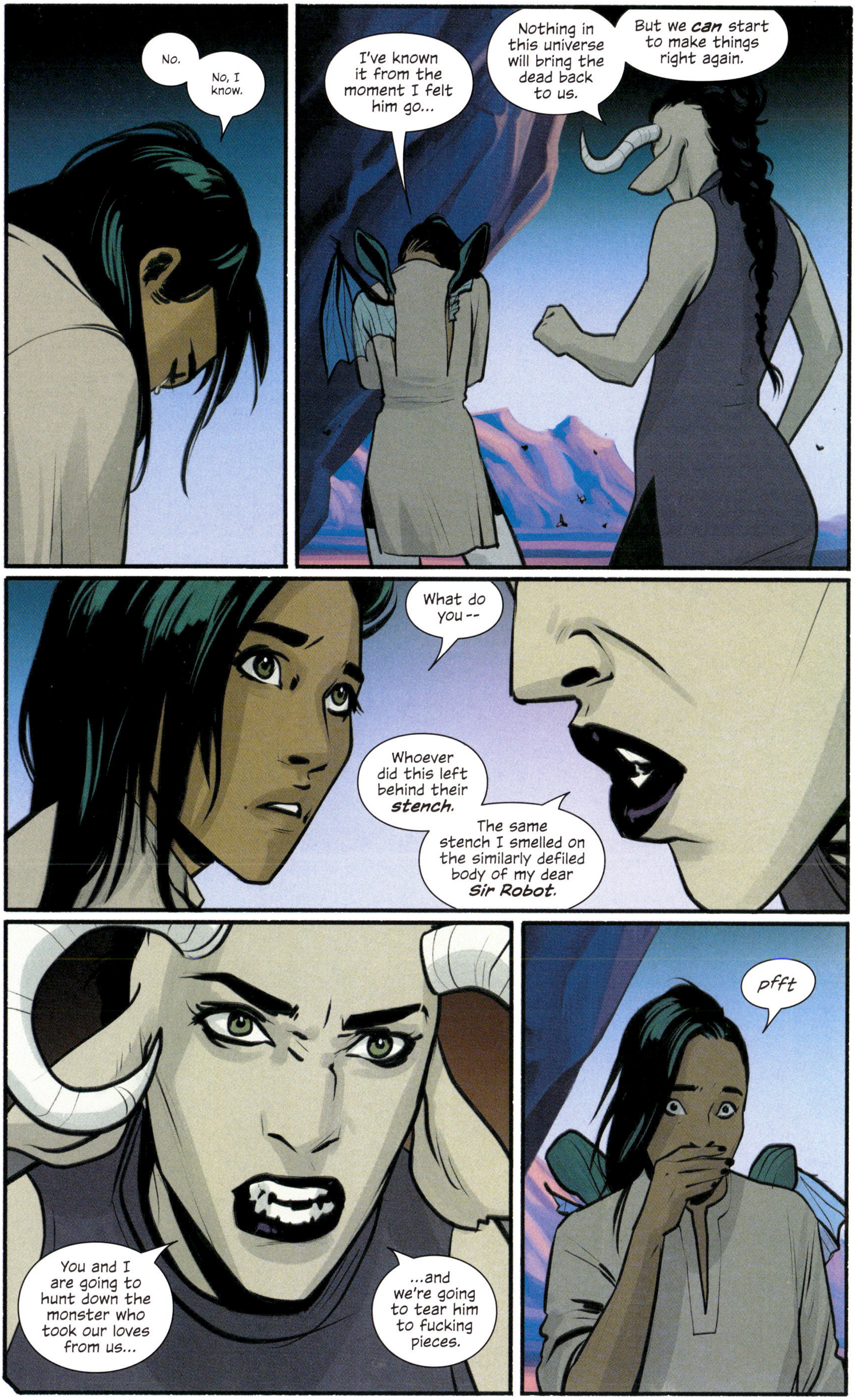
No.
No, I know.
I've known it from the moment I felt him go...
Nothing in this universe will bring the dead back to us.
But we *can* start to make things right again.
What do you--
Whoever did this left behind their *stench*.
The same stench I smelled on the similarly defiled body of my dear *Sir Robot*.
You and I are going to hunt down the monster who took our loves from us...
...and we're going to tear him to fucking pieces.
pfft

heh
Haa.
AhaHaHaHaHaHa
I... don't understand what's happening here.
Heh, sorry, but dedicating the rest of my life to some dopey blood feud is literally the last thing Marko would have wanted.
Hell, it's why whatever pathetic zilch killed my husband left a trail, hoping we'd be idiotic enough to follow.
So what, Alana? You plan to let his murderer go unpunished? To just give up on ever finding justice?
...
Guess that about sums it up, yeah.

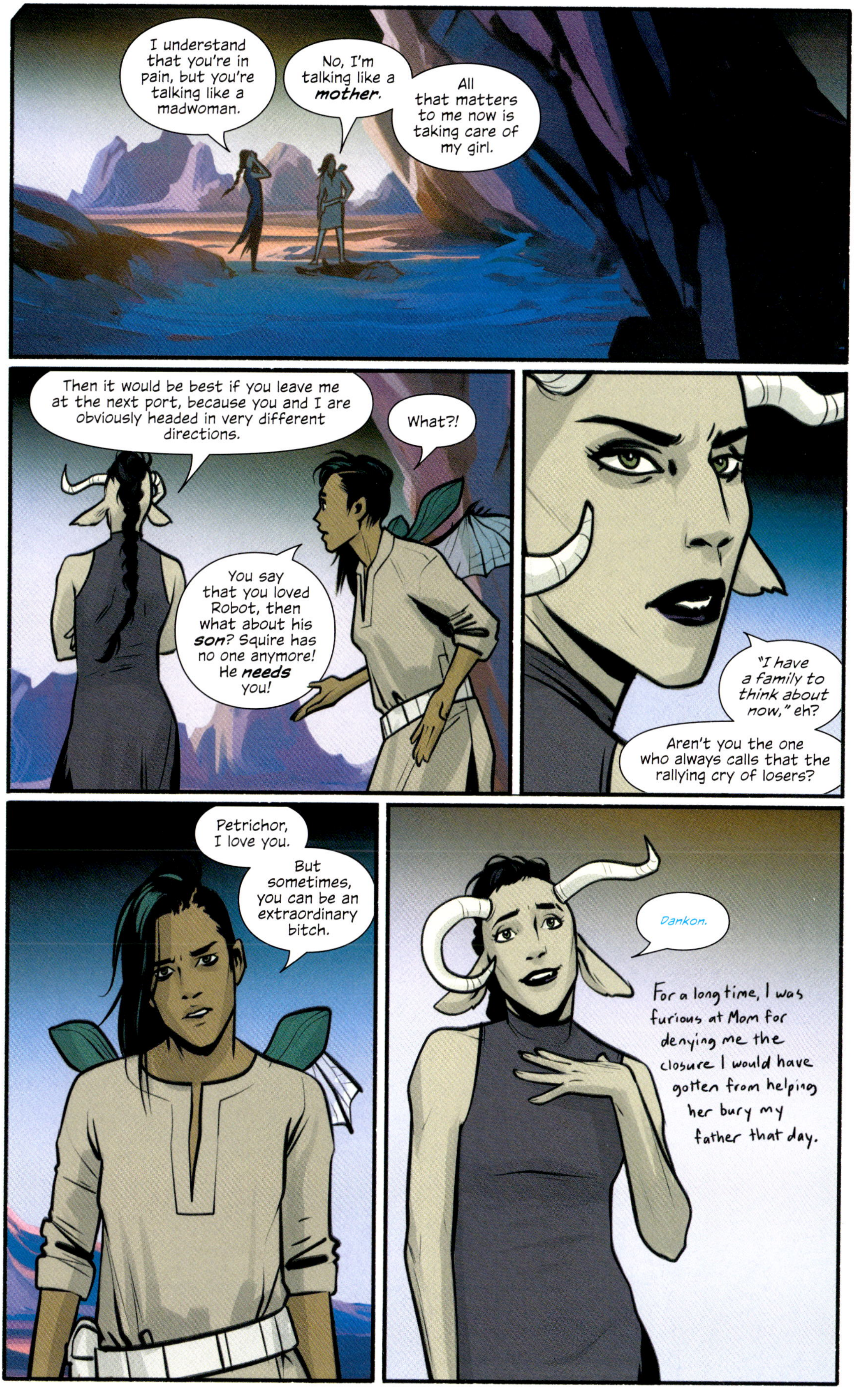

I understand that you're in pain, but you're talking like a madwoman.
No, I'm talking like a *mother*.
All that matters to me now is taking care of my girl.
Then it would be best if you leave me at the next port, because you and I are obviously headed in very different directions.
What?!
You say that you loved Robot, then what about his *son*? Squire has no one anymore! He *needs* you!
"I have a family to think about now," eh?
Aren't you the one who always calls that the rallying cry of losers?
Petrichor, I love you.
But sometimes, you can be an extraordinary bitch.
Dankon.
For a long time, I was furious at Mom for denying me the closure I would have gotten from helping her bury my father that day.

It took me a lifetime to learn that some doors just can't be closed.
You're saying you have the power to, what... *resurrect* my husband?
It's not about power, it's about resources.
Get me the right ones, and there's *nothing* I can't undo.
I appreciate that, Vitch.
Sincerely.
But I think I'll pass.

For real?
If you're worried he's gonna come back as some kind of shambling zombie, I guarantee this enchantment is nothing like that.
I hear you, but see, my guy, ***Murray***, he, *ah*, he drank himself to death.
Much as I miss the bastard, if I brought him back now, it'd only be a matter of months before I lost him all over again.
Gotcha.
Well, if you're still interested in getting out of this suburban hellscape, I can make you a phony travel pass for... let's say five grand.
Apiece?
It's my friends and family rate, 'cause you've been such a good customer.
Right.
Well, let me see what I can scrape together.
And if you ever change your mind about Murray, you know where to find me.

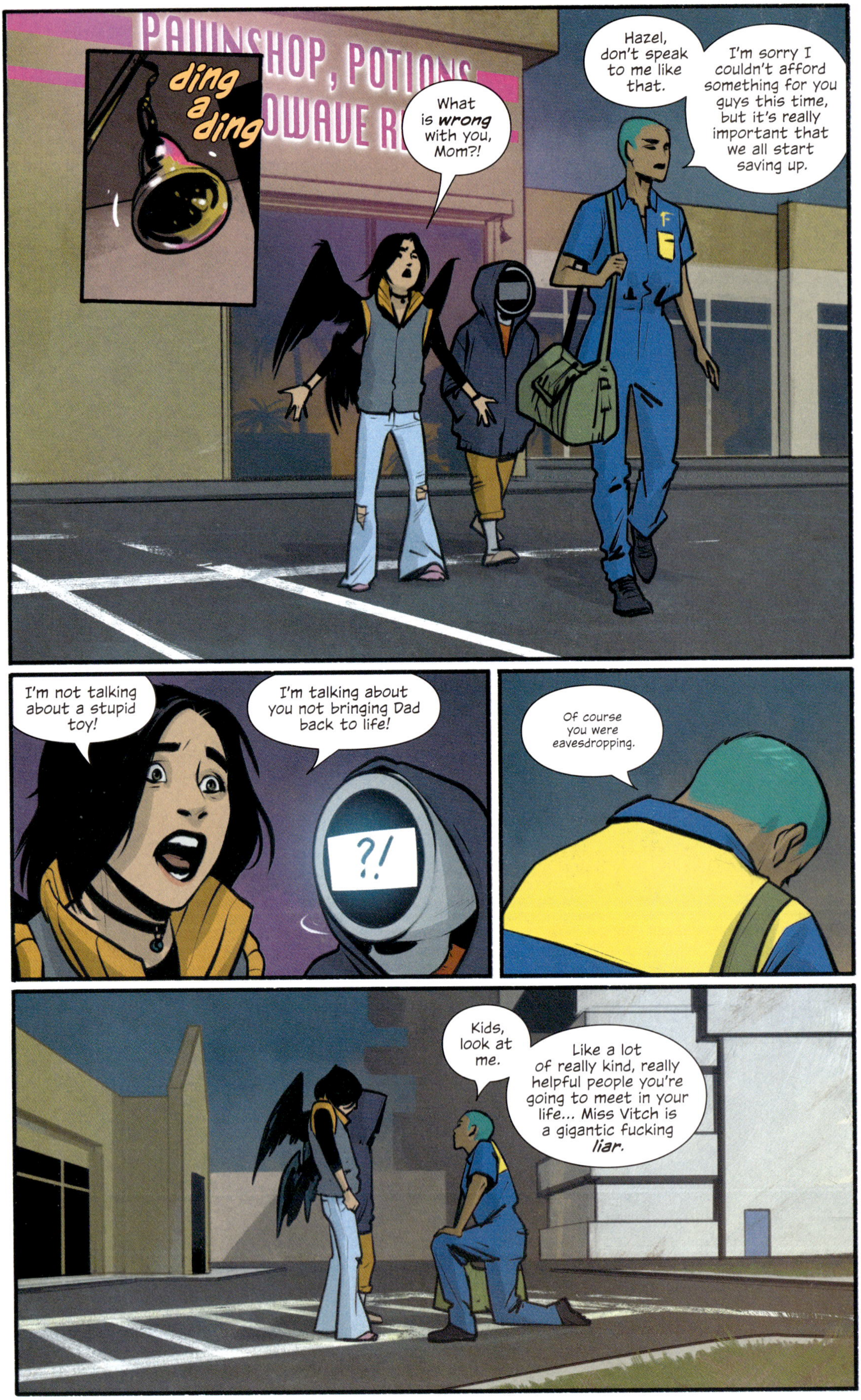
PAWNSHOP, POTIONS
ding a ding
What is *wrong* with you, Mom?!
Hazel, don't speak to me like that.
I'm sorry I couldn't afford something for you guys this time, but it's really important that we all start saving up.
I'm not talking about a stupid toy!
I'm talking about you not bringing Dad back to life!
?!
Of course you were eavesdropping.
Kids, look at me.
Like a lot of really kind, really helpful people you're going to meet in your life... Miss Vitch is a gigantic fucking *liar*.

Nuh-uh!
She said this necklace would change the way I look, and it totally hides my you-know-whats!
That's how liars work, sweetheart.
They earn your trust by giving you truth after truth.
And then, one day, they tell you something you really, really want to believe... and that'll be the whopper that does you in.
If there were any way I could give either of you your father back, I swear on all that's holy, I would.
But deep down, you both know that's just make-believe, right?
Okay then, little loves.
Time for Secret Book Club.
This next chapter is my favorite...

That doesn't belong to you, does it?
Sophie.
I... didn't know you could still hear old junk like you used to.
Most objects' *"voices"* are barely a whisper to me these days, but that ring certainly sounds like it was once owned by ***Gwendolyn***.
Yep.
Took it off the corpse of her no-good ex.
Then, why haven't you given it to her yet?

Intend to.
Just waiting for the right moment.
Oh, god.
You're planning to *propose*?
Well, it's something I've been contemplatin', but only after Gwen settles up with Velour and whatnot.
Judging by your mug, I'm guessing you don't approve.
Hmn.
You know, I've blocked out most of what I endured while a slave to Sextillion, but there's not a day that goes by that I don't think about one moment...
...when you caved in the skull of my captor.
Soph, I'm sorry as hell you ever had to bear witness to --
There's no need to apologize, The Will.
Most nights, replaying that memory is the only thing that gets me to sleep.

I learned a very valuable lesson that day.
The knowledge that someone who grievously wronged us has been snuffed from this mortal coil doesn't exactly bring one peace...
...but it ain't nothing.
Precisely.
And knowing how much pain this Marko person caused, I suspect your actions have been equally beneficial to my beloved guardian.
MRRRRN
You certainly don't need my blessing to ask for Gwendolyn's hand, but when the time comes, know that you have it.
Until then, this stays between us.
Young lady, I... I don't deserve someone like you in my life.
Lying.
WILL!

Get out of here!
Gwen? What's--
Just go!
Get as far away as possible, and take Lying Cat with you!
Should I leave as well, ma'am?
No, I'll need your help with preparations.
For what?
The last motherfucker I ever expected to see here.
As always, the rich and powerful continued to worry about whatever the hell it is the rich and powerful have to worry about.

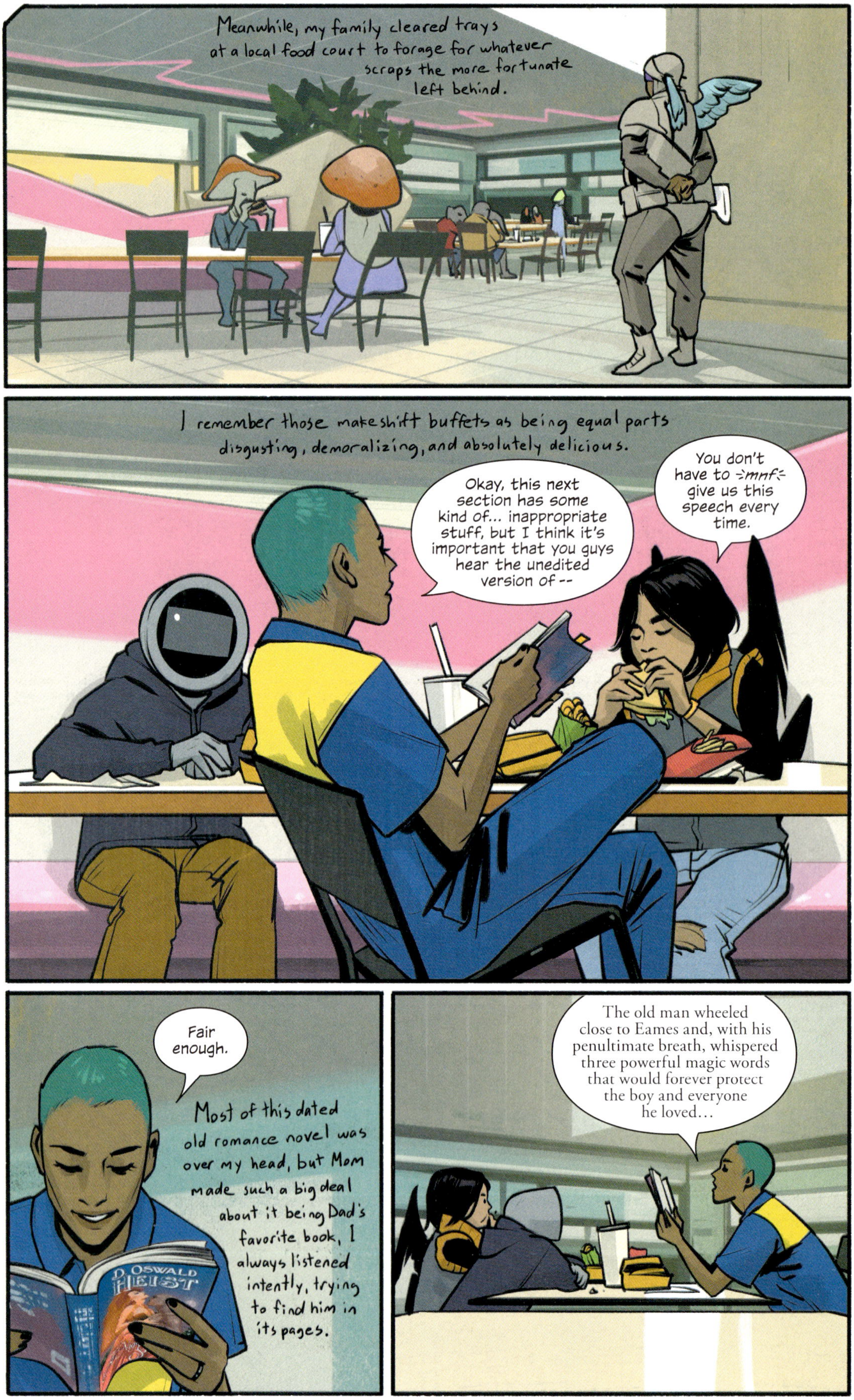
Meanwhile, my family cleared trays at a local food court to forage for whatever scraps the more fortunate left behind.
I remember those makeshift buffets as being equal parts disgusting, demoralizing, and absolutely delicious.
Okay, this next section has some kind of... inappropriate stuff, but I think it's important that you guys hear the unedited version of --
You don't have to =mnf= give us this speech every time.
Fair enough.
Most of this dated old romance novel was over my head, but Mom made such a big deal about it being Dad's favorite book, I always listened intently, trying to find him in its pages.
D. OSWALD
HEIST
The old man wheeled close to Eames and, with his penultimate breath, whispered three powerful magic words that would forever protect the boy and everyone he loved…

"Revenge… is… retarded."
D. OSWALD
HEIST
Ew!
Why the heck would you read that to us?!

Hang on, if you're offended, let's have a discussion why.
No!
I don't care what's written in your dumb book, we don't *use* that word anymore!
Especially not in front of a kid who's been *called* it!
I know now that Mom genuinely believed reading her son this story might eventually help save his life... but she was too late.
Squire had already finished "A Nighttime Smoke" on his own, twice.
He thought it opened okay but got boring in the middle, and even its most "shocking" parts were just more meaningless talk.
In the real world, all that mattered was action.

Honey, I'm *hooooome!*
Sorry I'm late, traffic was a complete...

Hello, Ginny.
Please... take whatever you want.
Oh, thanks ever so much, but I'm afraid I'm not some garden-variety home intruder.
Special Agent Gale, Landfall Secret Intelligence.
Wait, is this about *Marko?*
I... I haven't heard from him in *years*.

No, I can't imagine you have.
But I'm actually here about **another** trouble-maker who may have paid you a visit, an alleged journalist by the name of **Upsher**.
Help me find him, and I give you my word no harm will befall you **or** your charming family.
The amphibious guy?
Yeah, he... he gave me a **runestone**, told me I could use it to summon him anytime.
Splendid!
Oh, Ginny, you have no idea how much easier that makes my...

YAAAAHH!
NggghyougoddamnASSCUNT!
Baby, I love you!
Remember that Mama loved you so --
ZUPP

MMMNNNHH!
HWAHHH
ngh
For what little it's probably worth to you two... I think the old girl... made the right play there...

You were never getting out of this alive.
ZUPP ZUPP

end chapter sixty-two

CHAPTER

SIXTY-THREE

My little brother thinks you can raise the dead but that's just made-up bullshit.
Correct?

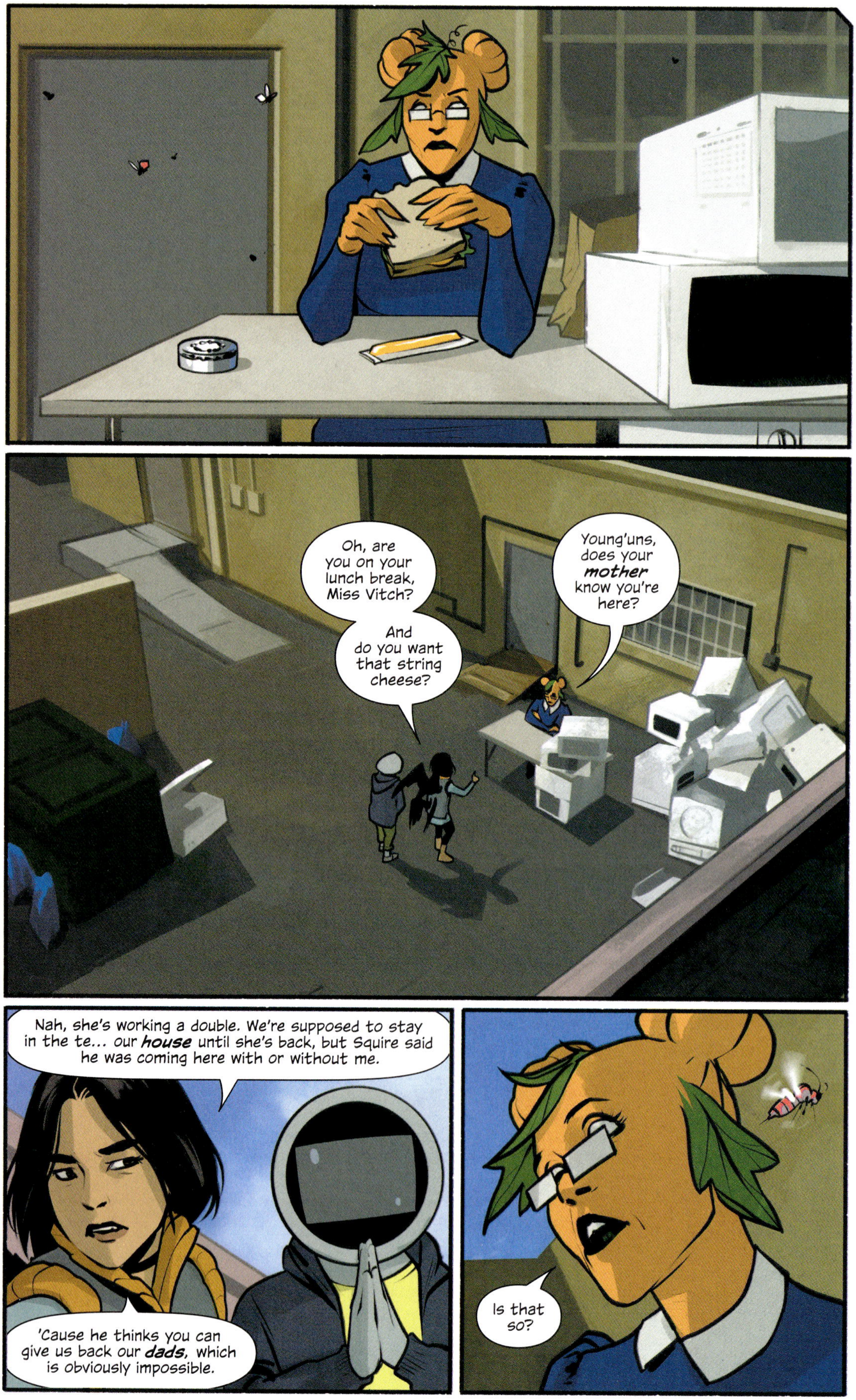
Oh, are you on your lunch break, Miss Vitch?
And do you want that string cheese?
Young'uns, does your *mother* know you're here?
Nah, she's working a double. We're supposed to stay in the te... our *house* until she's back, but Squire said he was coming here with or without me.
'Cause he thinks you can give us back our *dads*, which is obviously impossible.
Is that so?

sfwack
Come.
Come closer, don't be scared, babies.
To answer your somewhat obnoxious question, no, I can't "raise the dead."
But with enough of *this*...
phhweww

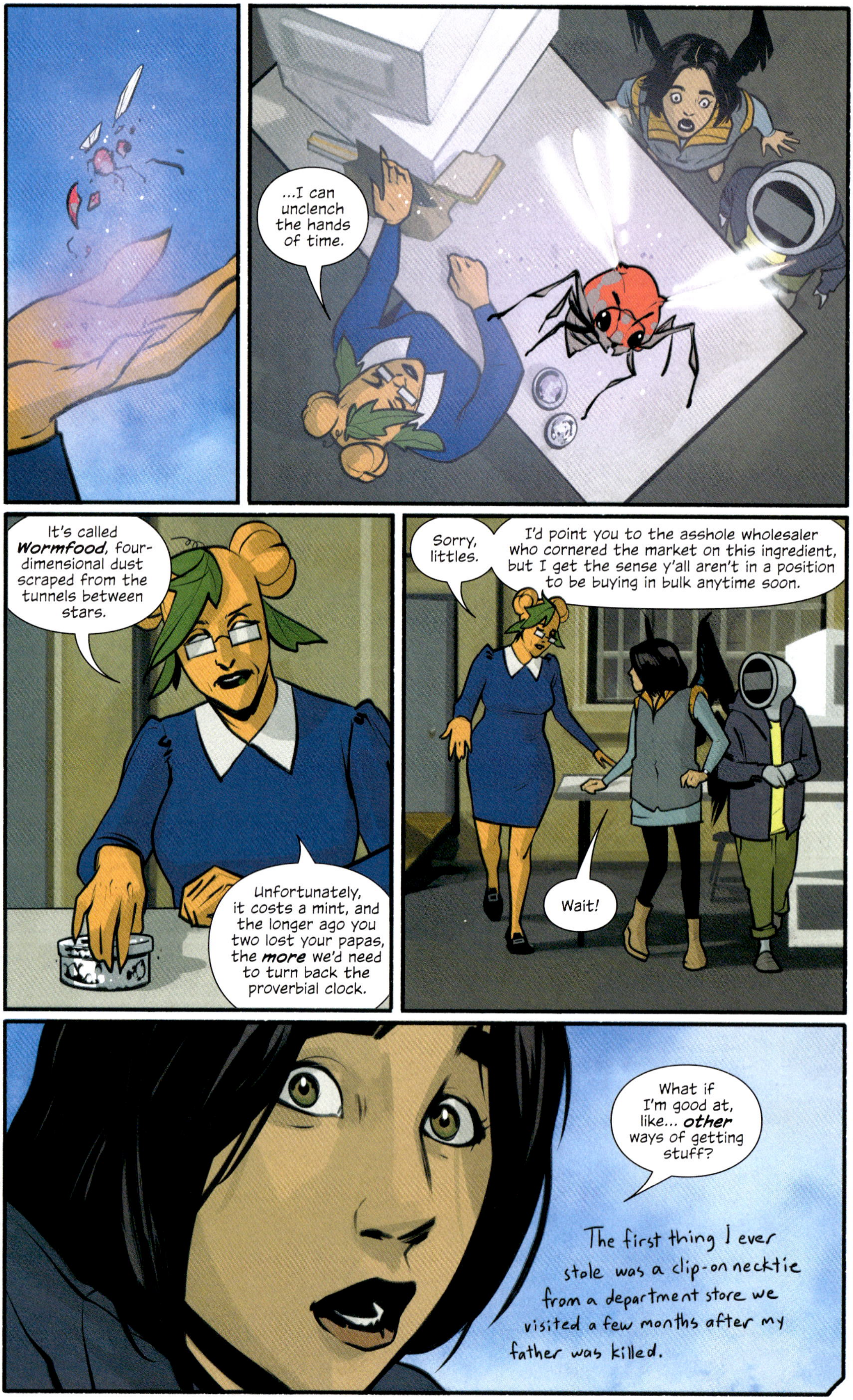
...I can unclench the hands of time.
It's called **Wormfood**, four-dimensional dust scraped from the tunnels between stars.
Unfortunately, it costs a mint, and the longer ago you two lost your papas, the **more** we'd need to turn back the proverbial clock.
Sorry, littles.
I'd point you to the asshole wholesaler who cornered the market on this ingredient, but I get the sense y'all aren't in a position to be buying in bulk anytime soon.
Wait!
What if I'm good at, like... **other** ways of getting stuff?
The first thing I ever stole was a clip-on necktie from a department store we visited a few months after my father was killed.

It wasn't so much about the object (even though it was awesome and could even be attached to t-shirts), it was about the FEELING of taking it, of breaking "the rules."
Airland
INN
No longer was I some powerless satellite controlled by others' gravity...
I was a goddamn star.
Petrichor, darling?

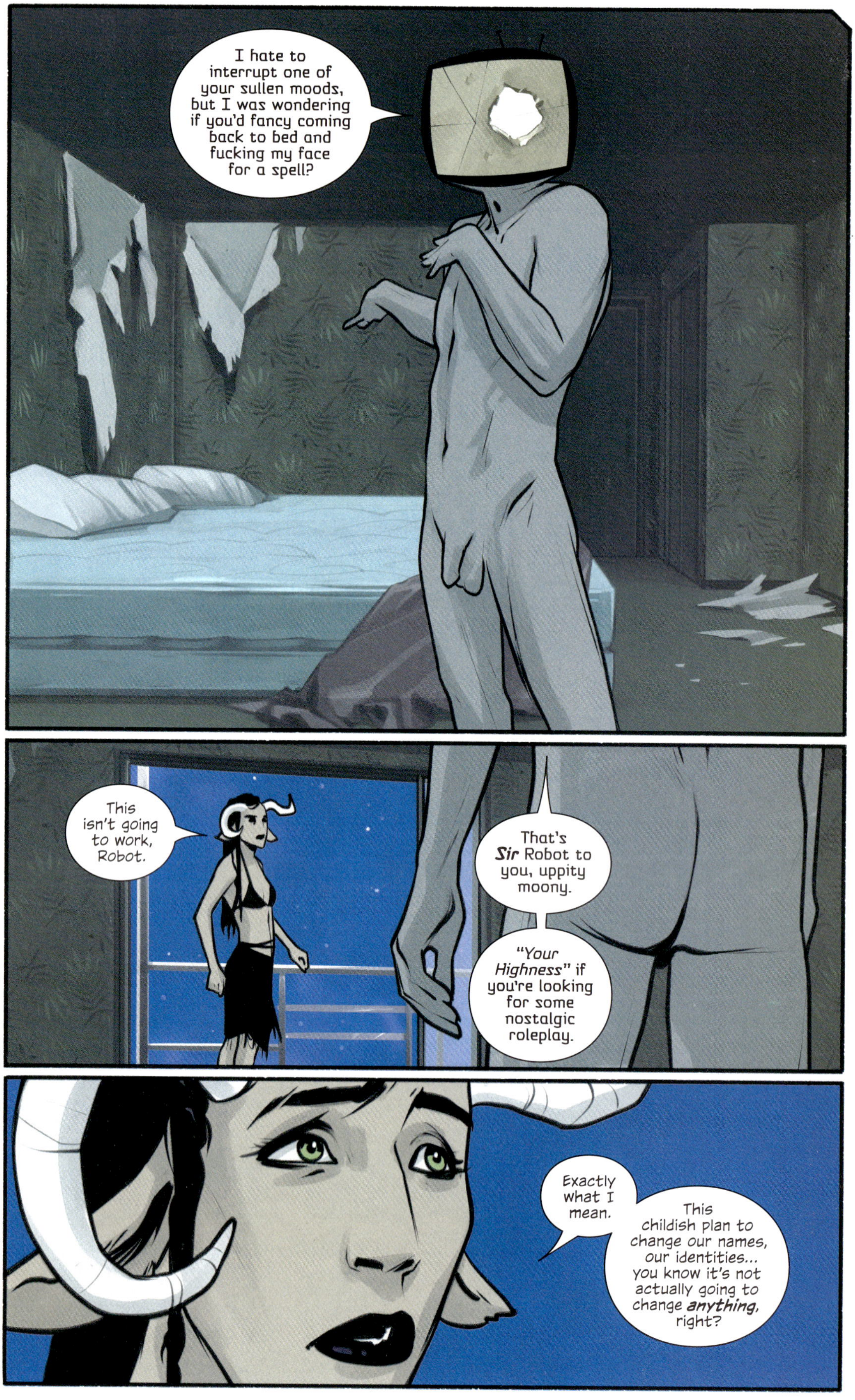
I hate to interrupt one of your sullen moods, but I was wondering if you'd fancy coming back to bed and fucking my face for a spell?
This isn't going to work, Robot.
That's *Sir* Robot to you, uppity moony.
"Your Highness" if you're looking for some nostalgic roleplay.
Exactly what I mean.
This childish plan to change our names, our identities... you know it's not actually going to change *anything*, right?

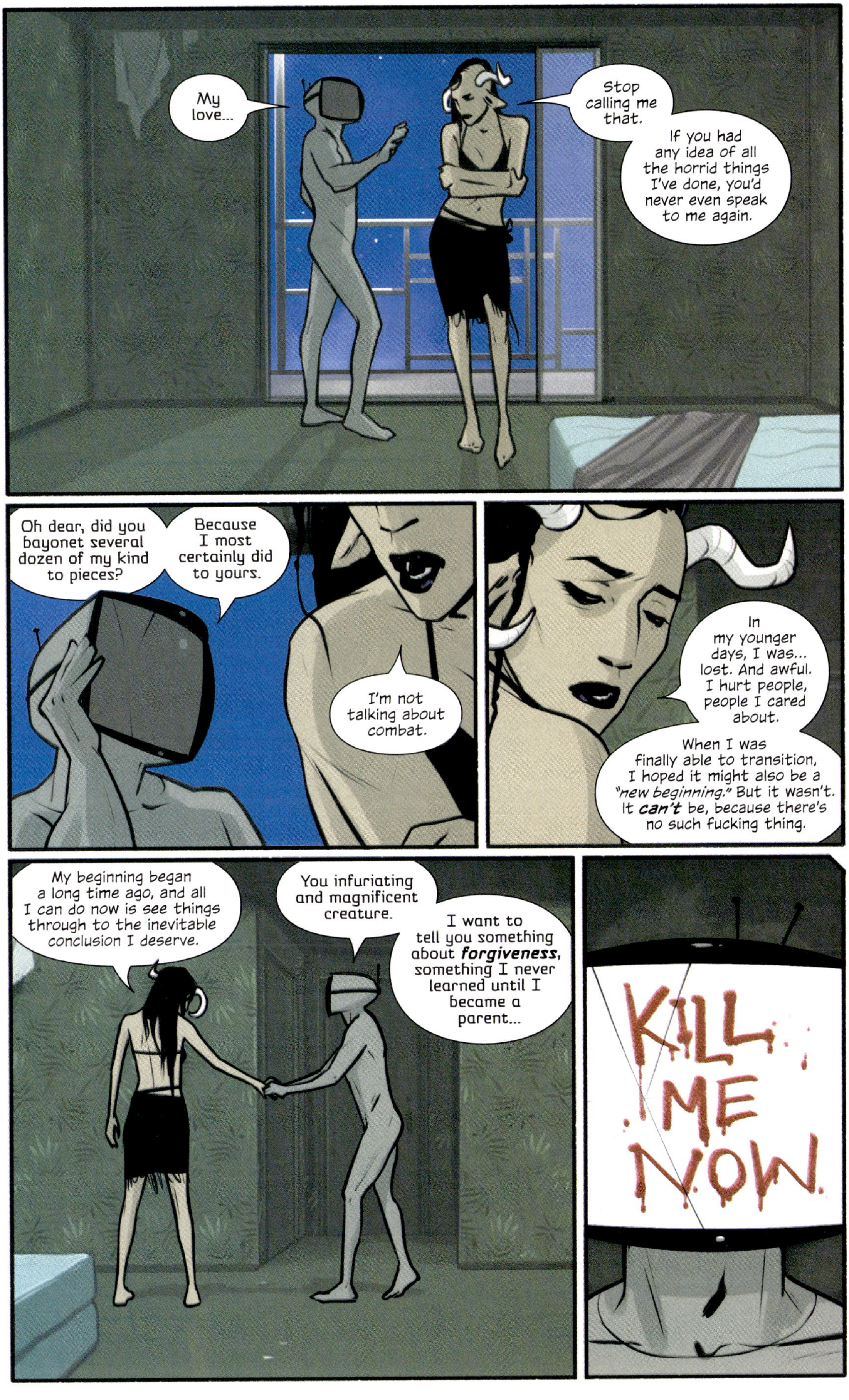
My love...
Stop calling me that.
If you had any idea of all the horrid things I've done, you'd never even speak to me again.
Oh dear, did you bayonet several dozen of my kind to pieces?
Because I most certainly did to yours.
I'm not talking about combat.
In my younger days, I was... lost. And awful. I hurt people, people I cared about.
When I was finally able to transition, I hoped it might also be a *"new beginning."* But it wasn't. It ***can't*** be, because there's no such fucking thing.
My beginning began a long time ago, and all I can do now is see things through to the inevitable conclusion I deserve.
You infuriating and magnificent creature.
I want to tell you something about ***forgiveness***, something I never learned until I became a parent...
KILL ME NOW.

Kio?
...please...
...I'm begging you...
...please just kill me now...
I'm not going to hurt you again, Erving.
So long as *The Will* is really where you say.

Lady, I'm sorry about what happened to your boyfriend, but there's a *system* in place for you to get restitution if a Freelancer did something out of bounds.
But you go to Wreath and try to settle this on your own, I guarantee The Will is gonna *dismember* you, and then he's gonna dismember *me* for sending you his way.
We'll see.
Listen, you ditzy broad!
A few years ago, sure, a well-armed Wreath soldier with the element of surprise *might* have stood a shot against the guy... but that was motherfuckin' then!
I don't know what happened while he was out of the union and in the wilderness, but The Will, he came back *different*, okay?
He's... he's sharper, more confident, like he finally knows exactly who and what he really is.
Which is?
Ehh, what's it matter?
We both know you're about to find out for yourself.

FULFILLMENT!
Hurry, #1211!
If a Floor Manager catches you away from the line again, you're gonna get canned!
Oh, no.
However would I go on if banished from this paradise?
WSSSSS

I know the hours suck, but have you ever worked a *call center*?
Compared to having to explain to old people how to use a new phone *over* the phone, this place *is* paradise.
You're a legend, Packer #729.
hyuh
Want to know my secret to success?
I'm high as a frickin' mongoose on *Fadeaway* right now.
You want a taste?
yes yes yes yes
I'm good, thanks.

Anyway, not like I'm looking to stay here until I get a gold watch or whatever.
I just need to save up enough to get my kids and me off this orbiting strip mall.
You really want to leave so bad, why not get a job on a *ship*?
Trust me, I'm down at the docks once a week looking for work.
Unfortunately, that industry doesn't seem particularly interested in hiring somebody who comes with her own passengers.
Well, maybe not the major lines that work with the wings or horns.
But on the boats that travel to places that haven't been forced to pick a side yet, I've heard the rules are a little more... lax.
You think they might let me bring children on board?
Depends.
How old are yours again?
Ten and almost twelve.
Oh, that's *more* than old enough for them to get paying work!

You mean *child labor*?
You say that like it's a bad thing. Most of the stuff we send out was *made* by little kids.
That doesn't make it any less fucked up!
I mean, my two pass the hat after they play their songs, but that's like letting them run a lemonade stand. You're talking about me forcing them into the adult workforce?
No, I might not be able to shield them from the war, but I can save them from this misery, at least for a while longer.
Shh, incoming.
How are we feeling, Fulfillment Family Members?
Fantastic!
Fantastic.
What *kind* of work would they be doing...?

How *old* is this, ma'am?
Haven't the faintest.
I just asked Wreath Archives to dig up whatever artwork hadn't been destroyed from the pre-Schism era.
I want to give **King Robot** a reminder that what he's bravely come here to do isn't a betrayal, but more of a... loving act of redemption.
Hmm.

Sophie, if you have concerns, kindly voice them now.
I'll admit, even before I became a proud citizen of your moon, I held certain prejudices against the bluebloods.
They were some of the most vicious "customers" I survived while in captivity, though I recognize those monsters might not represent their entire extended kingdom.
And yet... a kingdom?
High Command is really prepared to get back in bed with a monarchy, a hereditary one, only the most absurd form of governance ever --
kzzsssssst
TSSSPOPP
Malbona posttagmezon... mi venas... en pecoj.
Did I get any of that rubbish anywhere close to correct?

The fuck are you supposed to be?!
Take a breath, Gwendolyn.
Why start an interstellar incident before we've been properly introduced?
I was assured I'd been granted an audience with the King, not one of his harem girls.
My title is Countess Robot X, but when I wield his scepter, I speak and act with the full authority of the one true sovereign.
And he's had more than enough of your gifted skulls and other veiled overtures, so let's fast-forward past the foreplay and get to the facial.
BITCH PLEASE
Hn.
The first document my page has for you is an official non-aggression pact, effective the moment His Majesty -- or one of his vulgar representatives -- signs it.
Are you completely fucking mental?
If we call a truce with you horns, the rest of the Coalition -- especially that boulder your pebble circles -- will take it as a declaration of war.
If you actually believed the "Coalition" were anything but a myth, would you really be standing on lunar soil right now?

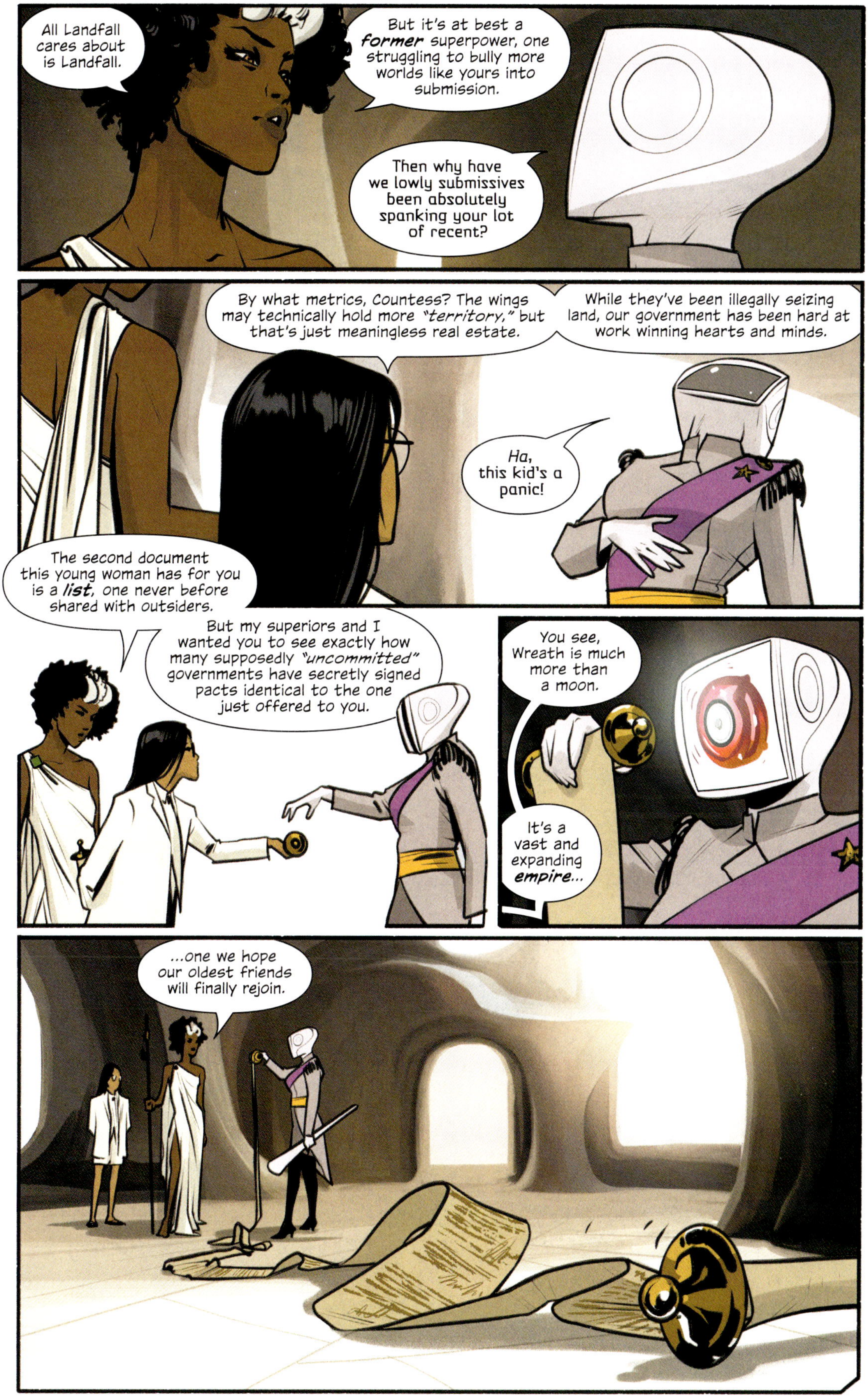
All Landfall cares about is Landfall.
But it's at best a **former** superpower, one struggling to bully more worlds like yours into submission.
Then why have we lowly submissives been absolutely spanking your lot of recent?
By what metrics, Countess? The wings may technically hold more *"territory,"* but that's just meaningless real estate.
While they've been illegally seizing land, our government has been hard at work winning hearts and minds.
Ha, this kid's a panic!
The second document this young woman has for you is a ***list***, one never before shared with outsiders.
But my superiors and I wanted you to see exactly how many supposedly *"uncommitted"* governments have secretly signed pacts identical to the one just offered to you.
You see, Wreath is much more than a moon.
It's a vast and expanding ***empire***...
...one we hope our oldest friends will finally rejoin.

Sure, no prob.
I've shop-lifted from scarier places than this.
WARNING: THIS GATE IS HEXED
Don't freak, those signs are always just for show.
And as long as we stay close together, Vitch said my new ***charmed bracelet*** will static out any cameras pointed in our direction.
We're, like, invisibler than ever.

Okay, hang on.
Petrichor once showed me how to *lightning* these things open.
Who *cares* if the spell takes time off my life?
We'll just use whatever Wormfood we grab to get it back, just like we're gonna get back our dads, my babysitter, Doff, *everybody*.
LYING

HSSSSS
mommy

People always say they'd be willing to "beg, borrow or steal" to get whatever they want most... but those were activities I used to do for fun.
To get my father back, I would have happily given up my own life.

My brother was willing to take it a step further.

end chapter sixty-three

CHAPTER

SIXTY-FOUR

Hello, my name's Pete.
I was hoping I could borrow just a moment of your time?

Sorry, fella.
I already gave at the office.
Oh, I'm not looking for a handout, I'm looking for a **woman**, a native of Landfall who may be going by the name **Alana**.
And you happen to match the description of an individual who was seen in her company on a planet near --
Not this racist shit again!
I don't know what kinda shady debt-collection outfit keeps sending you assholes my way, but I'll tell you the same thing I told the other guy.
One: I don't run with wingnuts, no offense. Two: half the dudes from my homeland rock a tricorne, so your ignorant assertion about somebody matching my --
Just a moment.
What *"other guy"* are you referring to?
DINER

Like his name? I don't remember, Upland or something?
But he was a fellow amphibian, which made his assumptions all the more galling, dig?
This individual, did he happen to give you anything? His card?
A runestone, perhaps?
Nah, just told me to keep an eye out for this Llama chick you're all horny for.
Rambled about a "big reward" if I steered her his way.
Hold on, he told you where to find him?
Yeah, but I wasn't exactly paying attention.
Think he maybe said something about a lighthouse?
A...?

Dranken?
I pinch a quick loaf and you already made new friends?
Hardly.
Creep was asking after you-know-who.
Fuuuuuck, what'd you say?
Exactly what that crazy mama *told* us to if trouble came calling.
Hope she knows what she's doing.
I just hope her kid's taking care of my guitar.
Sorry. I wasn't.

And yet, the friends and even acquaintances my family left in our wake continued risking their lives to take care of me.
What the hell did I ever do to deserve them?
Are you all right, Hazel?
...and now you talk?!

fshazzt
Shh.
Let's get the wormfood and go.
Squire.
You... you *killed* something.
Something, not someone.
But like, a *big* something.
A big something that *spoke*.
You're welcome for saving your life.
I just... didn't know you could... you know...
Neither did I.
But it felt quite... natural.

Right, here we are then.
Exactly where Miss Vitch said it would --
I'll be goddamned.
She's really sending kids to do her dirty work.
Easy, small fries.
I don't want to hurt anyone, but pull whatever pea shooter you used on that guard cat, I roast you alive.
Who...?
Lucky for you two, I'm one of the good guys.

Evening!
A colleague of mine told me your outfit might be open to hiring folks lacking certain **paperwork**, so I was hoping to --
Keep walking, slag.
Copy that, good sir.
Are you **kidding** me?!
You put your hands on my underage daughter?!
Boss, chill out for a second!
Me and your girl, we was just having a laugh!

Well, heck, I'm awful sorry then.
I had no idea you were merely joking around...
...with my motherlovin' *flesh and blood!*
WHUMP
hnnnnng
P.S., you're fired.
Get your junk off my boat before we pull up stakes.
Lords above.
Why is every chief of security also a secret piece of trash?
Maybe the people who help us most in life recognize a missing piece of themselves in us, something that has to be protected...

...or else they'll never be whole again.
SSSNNNIPPT

Malfermu.

THWAP
Ŝtelisto!
Hej, ĉesu!
Estas mi!
Petrografo...?
Ĉu vi vivas?

Petrografo mortis.
Mia nomo estas Petrichor.
Kiu zorgas?
Vi ankoraŭ estas mia infano.
Panjo...
La familia mort-komercisto.
Kial?
Venĝo.

Mia koro.
Feliĉa ĉasado.
No matter how many life-changing figures cross our paths, sooner or later, we supposedly all become our parents.

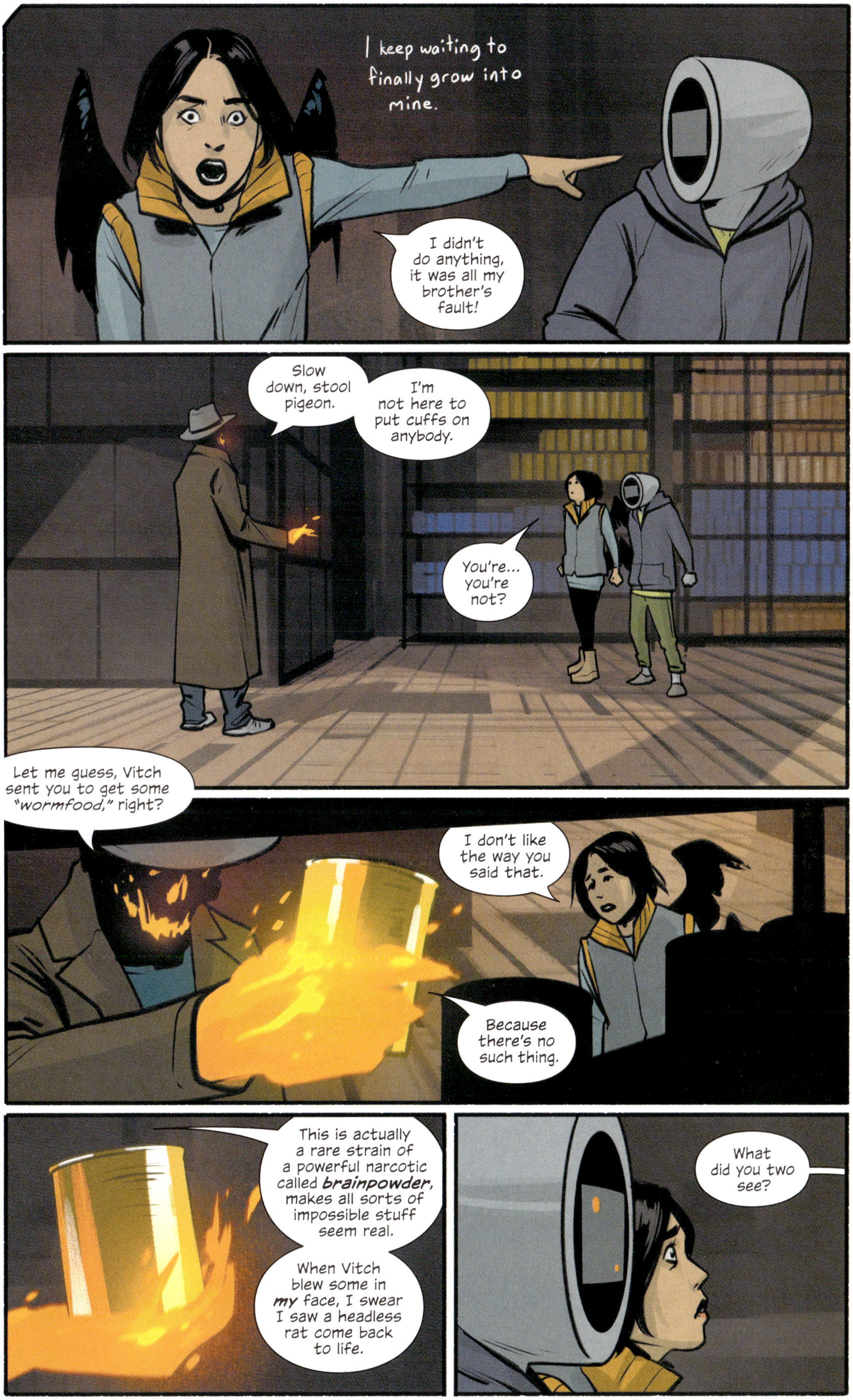
I keep waiting to finally grow into mine.
I didn't do anything, it was all my brother's fault!
Slow down, stool pigeon.
I'm not here to put cuffs on anybody.
You're... you're not?
Let me guess, Vitch sent you to get some "*wormfood*," right?
I don't like the way you said that.
Because there's no such thing.
This is actually a rare strain of a powerful narcotic called ***brainpowder***, makes all sorts of impossible stuff seem real.
When Vitch blew some in ***my*** face, I swear I saw a headless rat come back to life.
What did you two see?

Don't feel too bad.
I fell for it, and I'm a grown-ass man, one who's actually ***partied*** on stuff like this.
But me and my girl-friend, we lost our ***daughter*** a few years ago.
Backyard pool, stupid accident.
So when I met Vitch, and she told me the dead don't have to stay dead?
I was ready to do ***anything*** to get my little girl back.
Like, *um*, like what?
Some twisted stuff, kid.
Vitch asked me to do some pretty twisted stuff.
By the time I realized I'd been scammed, it was too late.
But you're a Constable!
If this is really all just a bunch of B.S., why don't you ***arrest*** her?

Vitch said if I ever tried to make a move against her, she'd tell my **bosses** everything I'd done.
That would send me straight to prison, which is the same thing as a death sentence for a guy in my line of work.
So yeah, I'm pretty much screwed.
But at least I can prevent **other** folks from making my dumb mistake, which is why I've been staking out Vitch's place, trying to head off her next victims.
Anyway, I'll do my best to cover your tracks before the psycho who owns this place shows up, but you two should split.
If we don't bring her what we promised, won't Miss Vitch, like, put a hex on us for life?
I'll tell her you guys got pinched by a plainclothes like me and sent to ***juvie***.
Lie low for a few weeks, she'll forget all about you and move on to some other poor saps.
Okay, yeah.
Yeah, thank you so much, that's ***exactly*** what we'll do.
Like bloody hell.

I don't believe a word this firebug just said.
Careful, junior.
Squire, what are you --
You and I are leaving here with all the wormfood we can carry...
...even if it's over this pig's dead body.

Excuse me, sir?
Sorry, darling.
Whatever my thieving ticket guy told you at the booth, we don't do refunds.
Actually, I wanted to offer my ***services***, in your security department?
This ain't a luxury cruise ship, it's a low-rent ***circus boat***.
I need a lug who can handle drunken passengers ***and*** the drunken carneys I employ.
Well, I did a little time in the Open Circuit, so I have plenty of experience with creative --
Forget that pampered crap.
You ever seen ***combat***?

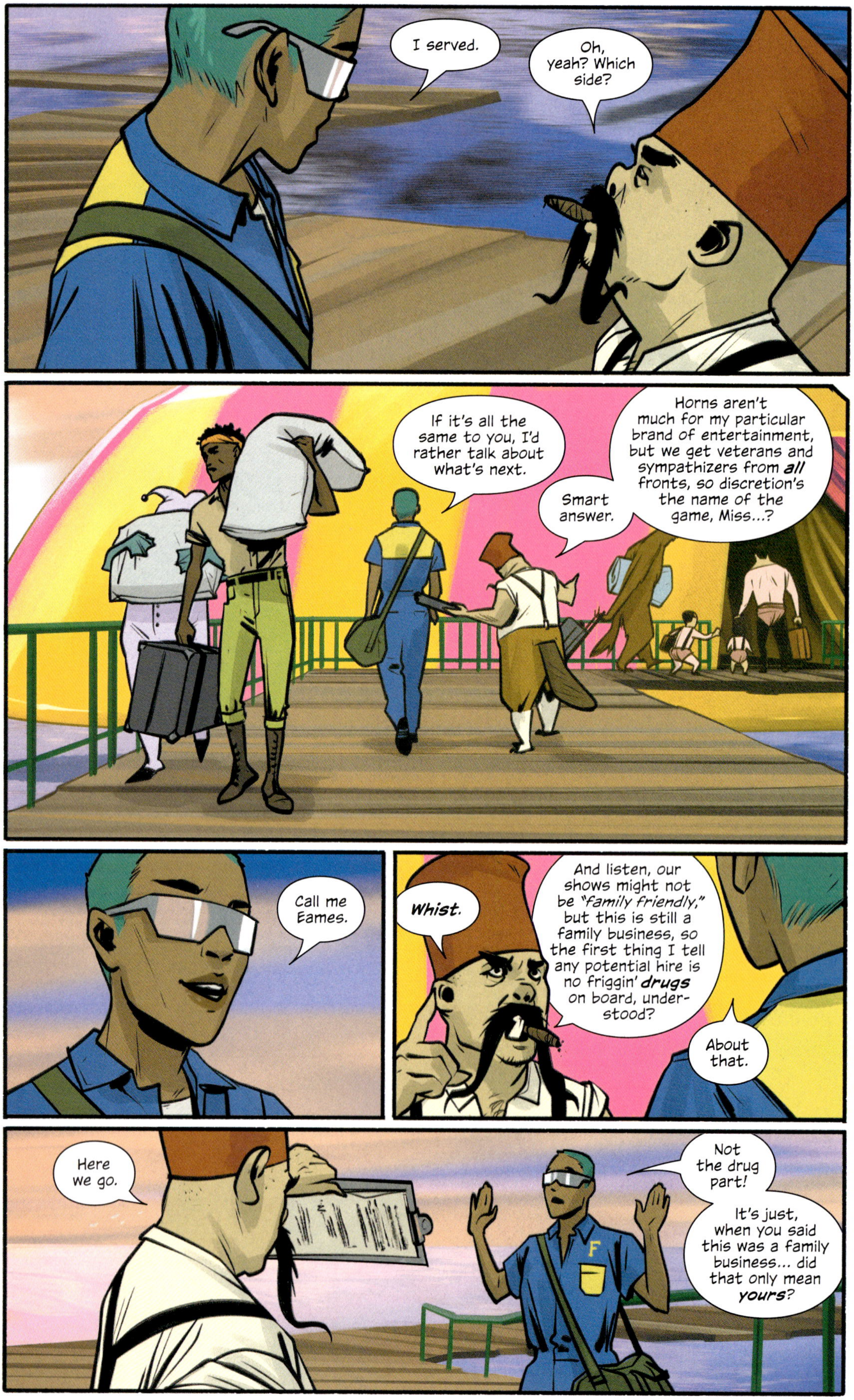
I served.
Oh, yeah? Which side?
If it's all the same to you, I'd rather talk about what's next.
Smart answer.
Horns aren't much for my particular brand of entertainment, but we get veterans and sympathizers from *all* fronts, so discretion's the name of the game, Miss...?
Call me Eames.
Whist.
And listen, our shows might not be *"family friendly,"* but this is still a family business, so the first thing I tell any potential hire is no friggin' *drugs* on board, understood?
About that.
Here we go.
Not the drug part!
It's just, when you said this was a family business... did that only mean *yours?*

Heavy sigh.
How big's your tribe?
Two preteens I adopted back on Phang.
Can they carry their weight?
Do you mean that literally or...?
Yes.
Yes, if it means three square meals and bunks without bedbugs, my children are one hundred percent willing and able to help.
Heh, they'll get a lot more than that.
But you'd better yank your youngsters out of whatever lousy daycare they're parked in, 'cause we blast off for our next world in thirty.
Thirty days?
Minutes.

That a problem?

end chapter sixty-four

CHAPTER

SIXTY-FIVE

When I was eleven, our front door had a zipper.
KIDS!
WE'RE MOVING!

Nights were hardest, with only that painfully thin membrane to protect us from every terrifying sound outside.
Kids...?

Still, Mom always assured my brother and me that our "camping adventure" would be over before we knew it.
Oh, fuck.

FUCK!
Until then, she encouraged us to remember one thing, that no matter how shitty our hardscrabble lives seemed...

...some poor bastards out there always had it worse.
"I'll think about it."
And that's all she said?
Actually, Countess X's exact parting words were, "We'll think about it."
An important distinction in the Robot Kingdom.
You should have seen Miss Gwendolyn in action. She was magnificent.
I don't doubt it.
But you ladies really think this one meet could turn the tide of the entire war?
Never forget that Wreath is a moon.
Turning tides is what we do.
EHHN EHHN EHHN EHHN

EHHN EHHN EHHN EHHN
The hell is that?
Exotic matter detector!
How?
Our security is *airtight.*
LYI--
And I get it, everything in life is relative, even suffering.

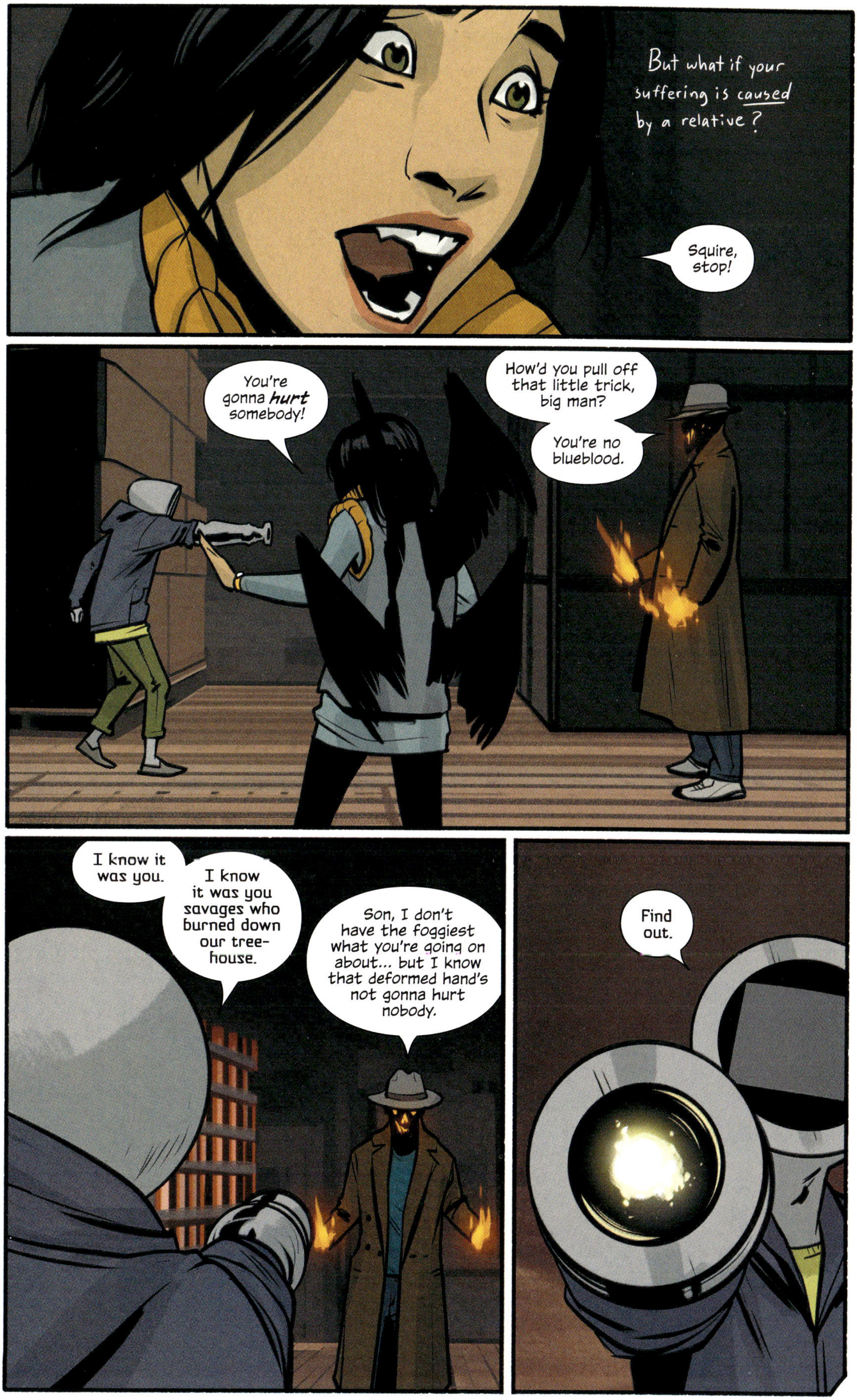
But what if your suffering is caused by a relative?
Squire, stop!
You're gonna hurt somebody!
How'd you pull off that little trick, big man?
You're no blueblood.
I know it was you.
I know it was you savages who burned down our tree-house.
Son, I don't have the foggiest what you're going on about... but I know that deformed hand's not gonna hurt nobody.
Find out.

DON'T!
...the fuck?
When did you turn completely psycho?!
nhf
And when did you *hnng* get so **heavy**?!

I'm only here for The Will.
The rest of you want to live, *leave.*
You *know* this asshole?
Never met her in my life.
Now get Sophie out of here.
We'll finish this.
HSSSSS
Legita!

MRAAAWR
L.C.!
Watch it, Will!
She brought a goddamn **death-merchant!**
Don't care if she brought an **army,** this bitch is --
KRAKK

HAZEL!
SQUIRE!
Yo.
You looking for the little girl and her drone?
Oh, god, yes, please!
Have you seen them?!
Maybe.
What's in it for me?

This is for Prince Robot IV, mother-fucker.
FULMO!
Nope.
GWENDOLYN!

We were so close!
We were so close, and you *ruined* it!
Now we'll *never* see our fathers again!
You're wrong, brobot.
Now that you tipped off the law about who you really are, we're *both* gonna see our dads again real soon.
'Cause you just got us *killed*!

I *warned* her.
I didn't want anyone else to get hurt. I just --
KLICK

OW
OW
You okay?
No.
Are you?
No...
KIDS!

...
You okay, Soph?
We're fine!
Just check on Miss --
Varmego.
TZZZZZZ
NYAAHH!!

Mom?
Are you all right?!
Why'd you leave the tent?!
Mom, we... we screwed up real bad.
Don't listen to her.
I'm the one who screwed up, Mom.
Oh.
Oh, my beautiful boy.
You sound *just* like your father.

NYAAAH!
...I was told... you were unstoppable...
...but you're nothing...
...but a *joke*...
twang

FASTER!
But our stuff!
Don't worry, I grabbed Daddy's pages and the drum-sticks Squire carved out of our old place and --
And my **guitar**?!
I kinda had to barter with it, but I swear I'll get you a new one.
For now, I need you both to be good helpers...
...and **KEEP UP!**

I did it.
NO!
I'm... I'm sorry.
I'm so sorry.

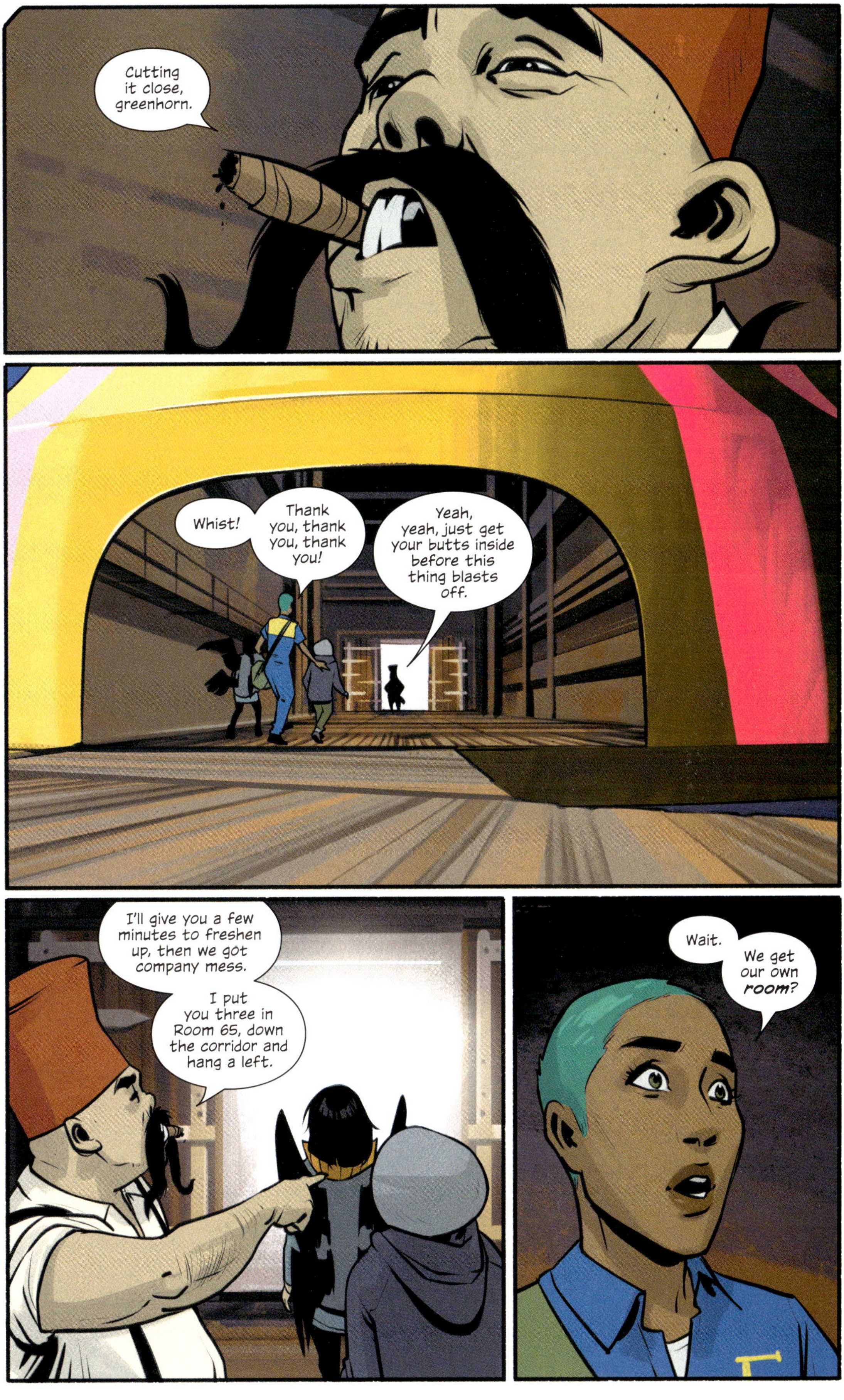
Cutting it close, greenhorn.
Whist!
Thank you, thank you, thank you!
Yeah, yeah, just get your butts inside before this thing blasts off.
I'll give you a few minutes to freshen up, then we got company mess.
I put you three in Room 65, down the corridor and hang a left.
Wait.
We get our own *room?*

It's all right, Gwen.
Thing only grazed her. She's gonna be fine.
LYING
That arrow.
Its poison has... no cure.
Soph?
SOPHIE!
Just because I was raised by pacifists doesn't mean my family wasn't constantly fighting.

We fought for resources, for shelter, for survival.
F
And thanks to the way Mom waged our battles, we sometimes even won.
But the close of that day was the first time since Dad's death that we'd managed to secure the most elusive of victories...

...an actual happy ending.

end chapter sixty-five

CHAPTER

SIXTY-SIX

How is it so far?

Huh?
Sorry to be a pest.
Just wondering if that novel's any good?
Ehn.
It's got one of those *"unreliable narrators,"* which always makes me worry the author's an asshole who's just making shit up as they go.
I. NEJAD GUEST
THE TRAPDOOR SPY
Oh, I actually quite like the device, when deployed correctly.
Have you ever read *Bell Weather?* It was shortlisted for the Hunziger Medal.
Yeah, I'm kind of allergic to books that win awards.
Heh.
Right.
Cool.

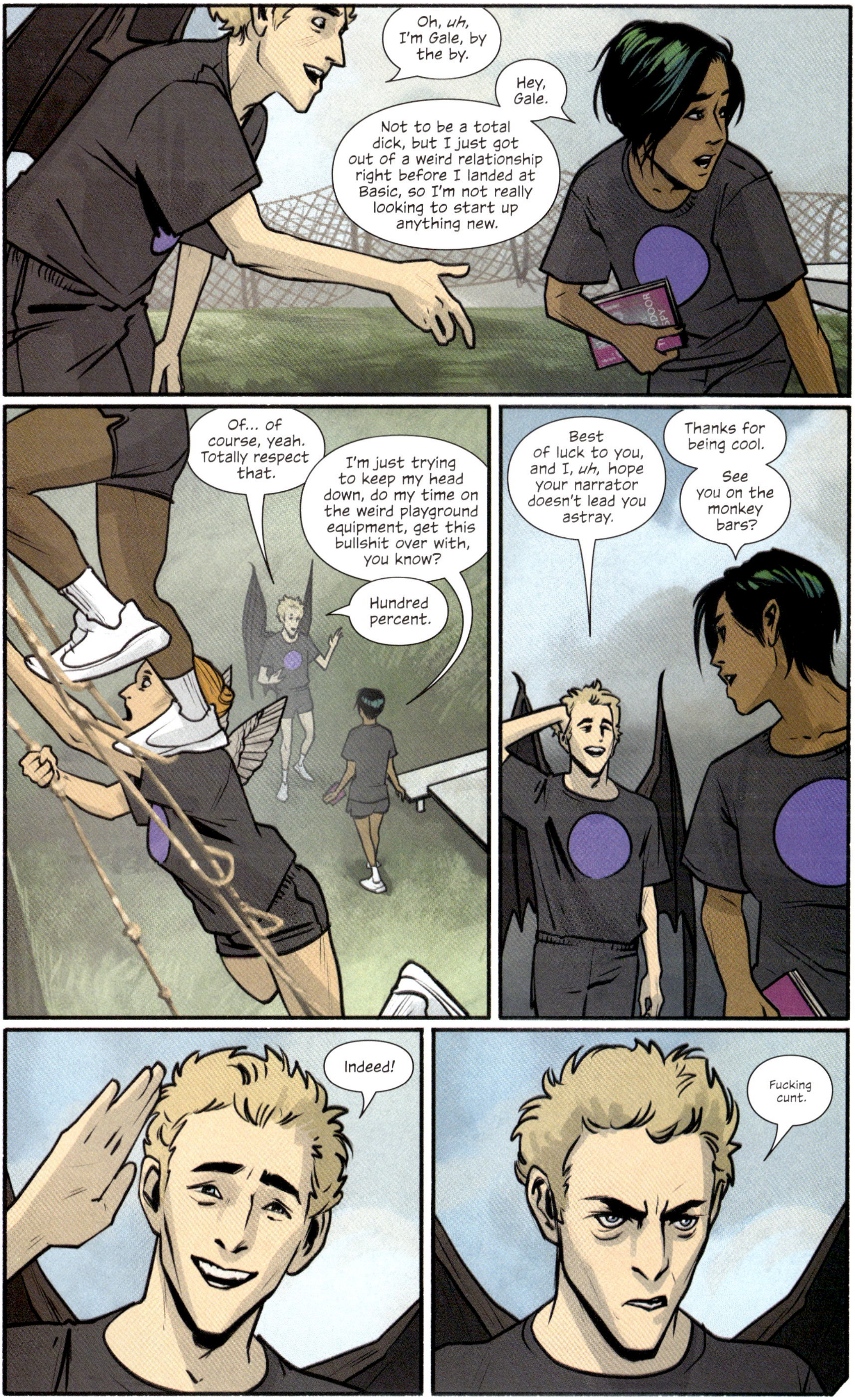

Oh, *uh*, I'm Gale, by the by.
Hey, Gale.
Not to be a total dick, but I just got out of a weird relationship right before I landed at Basic, so I'm not really looking to start up anything new.
Of... of course, yeah. Totally respect that.
I'm just trying to keep my head down, do my time on the weird playground equipment, get this bullshit over with, you know?
Hundred percent.
Best of luck to you, and I, *uh*, hope your narrator doesn't lead you astray.
Thanks for being cool.
See you on the monkey bars?
Indeed!
Fucking cunt.

MURRRR

D. OSWALD
HEIST
Night-Time
Smoke
Ugh.
Hello?!

Oh god, is somebody up there?!
Please!
Please, you have to hurry!
They'll be back soon!

You have to get me out of here!

...
Who the sweet fuck are you?

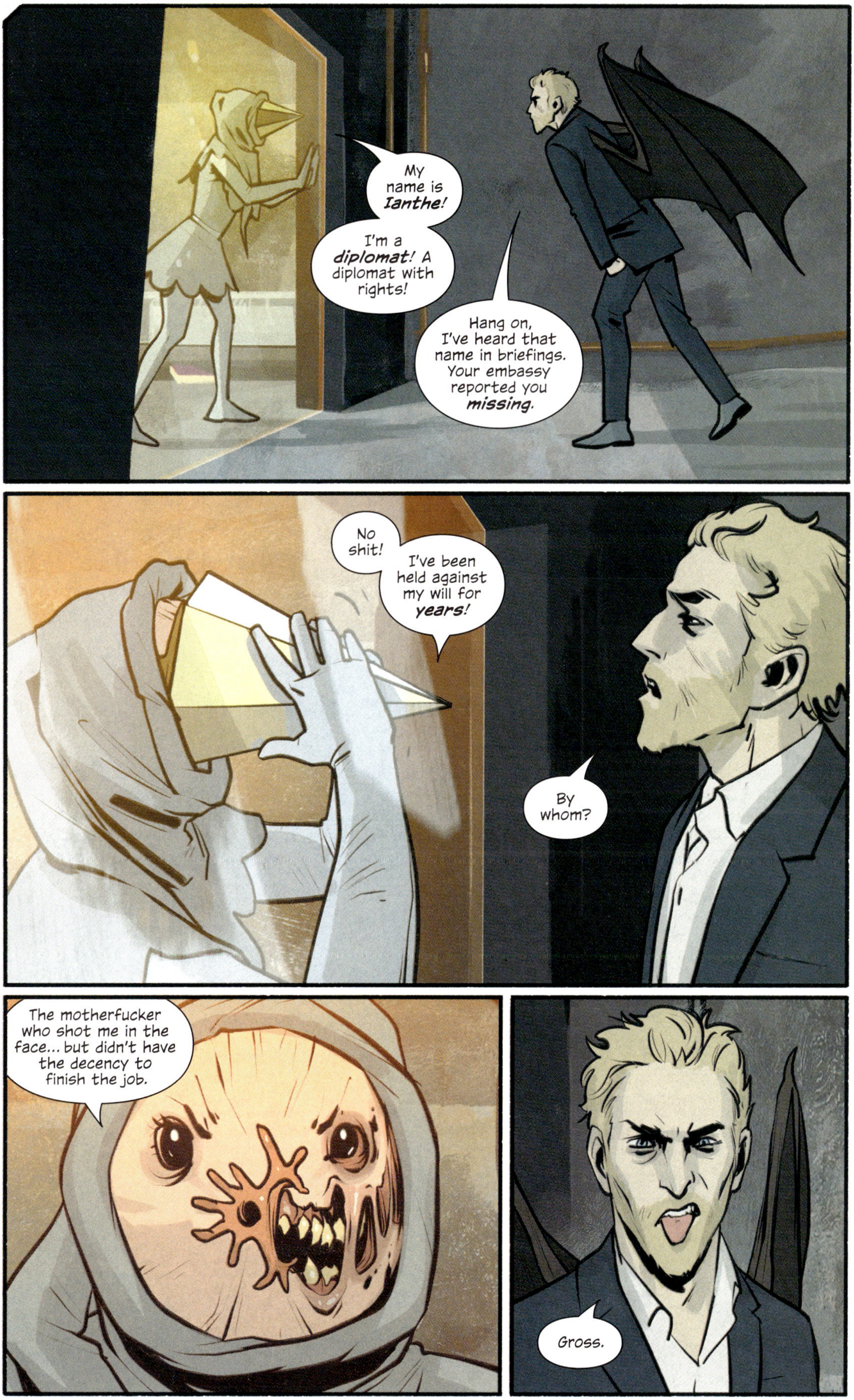

My name is *Ianthe!*
I'm a *diplomat!* A diplomat with rights!
Hang on, I've heard that name in briefings. Your embassy reported you *missing.*
No shit!
I've been held against my will for *years!*
By whom?
The motherfucker who shot me in the face... but didn't have the decency to finish the job.
Gross.

Anyway, I'd be happy to help secure your release, *if* you can tell me whether or not your captor has ever had a visit from...
...the hell?
FSSSSSSS
I *told* you to hurry.
nuh
nuh guh
buh

Whuh...?
Easy, fella.

One wrong move and Ghüs gives you a big ol' sad-hole.
Long time, Special Agent.

Upsher.
Listen to me very carefully: In a few minutes, you and this furry midget are both going to be *corpses*...
...unless you tell me exactly where to find Hazel and her whore of a mother.
Thankfully, I have no idea.
When we parted ways, everyone agreed it would be safest if the individuals you're looking for never told *anyone* of their whereabouts.
But Alana and her kin knew nogoodniks like you would still be hunting 'em, so she said she'd try to steer any bad fish straight into our net.
And by gum, looks like we finally caught one.
Yes, your capacity for strategy is awe-inspiring.
Say, isn't that what's-his-name... *Doff*?
Do tell, whatever happened to everyone's favorite shutterbug?

Did the worthless pieces of shit you're protecting manage to get *him* killed, too?
tak
My boyfriend was murdered by the woman you met downstairs.
Of course.
So you kept her alive to *torture* her.
Nuh-uh.
Upsher decided not to end that lady's life so she could be *rehabilitated*.
Well, that seems to be going swimmingly.
Breaking certain patterns can be... challenging.
Especially for someone suffering from the disease that afflicts Ianthe, me, our entire *culture*.
We're addicted to violence.

After I lost Doff, all I wanted to do was kill the woman who killed him.
But seeing the grace with which Alana responded to the horrific way she lost her partner... something changed in me.
I realized that -- hard as it may be to accept -- even someone like Ianthe has people who love her deeply.
Executing her only would have brought them gunning for me and everyone else I care about. So instead, I decided to break the cycle.
I came here to my new friend's home of Quietus, and as I nursed Ianthe back to health and rebuilt this old lighthouse brick by brick, I also rebuilt myself.
Taking a page from the author who used to call this place home, I developed a process where others could also unlearn the lessons of generational trauma.
Gale, I won't pretend to know what you've been through since we saw each other last... but I see in your eyes exactly what I saw in the woman who killed Doff.
You're not evil, you're powerless. And afraid. Whatever horrors you've been compelled to do -- by others or your own broken psyche -- it's not too late to start making amends.
It's not even too late to find redemption.

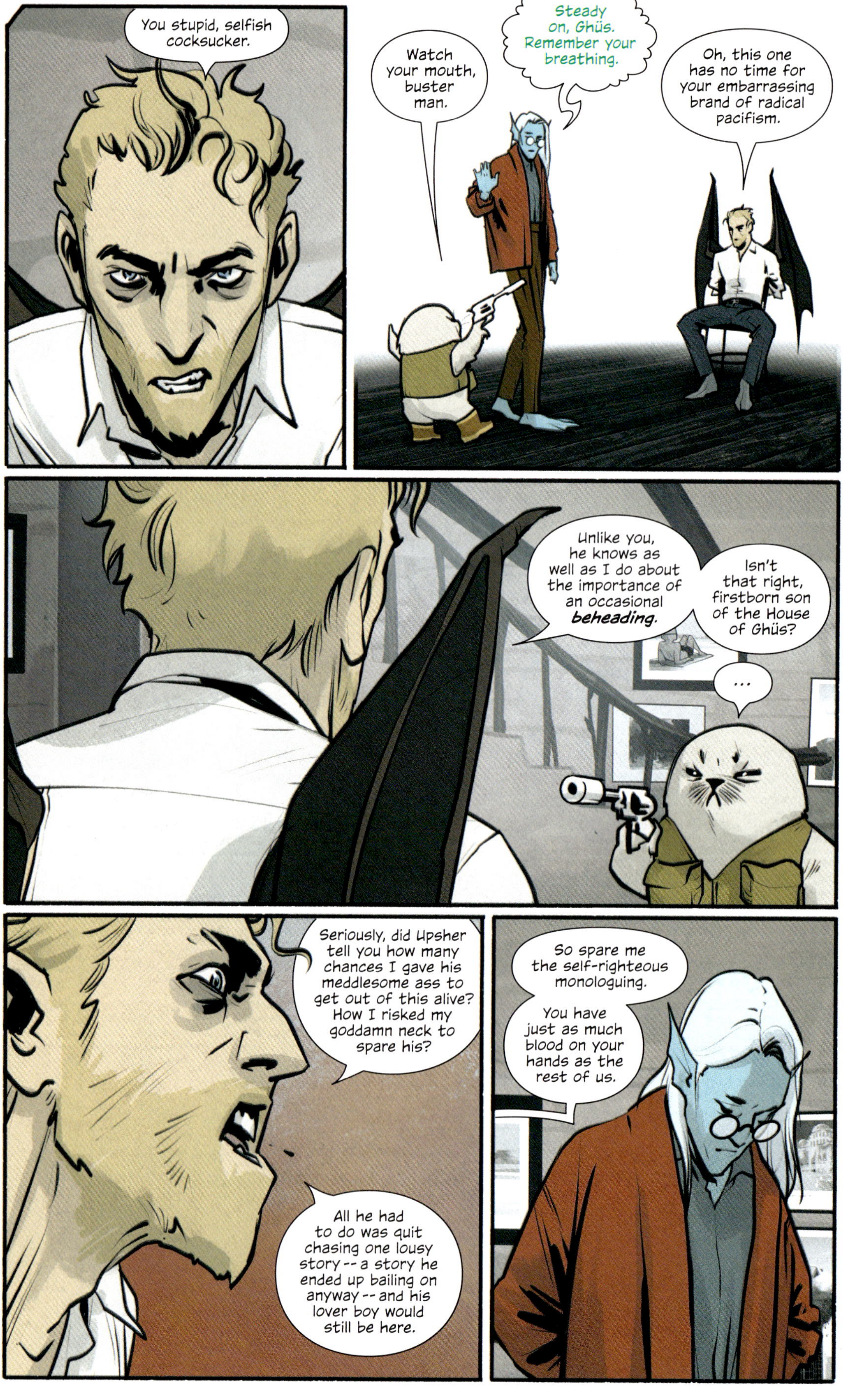

You stupid, selfish cocksucker.
Watch your mouth, buster man.
Steady on, Ghüs. Remember your breathing.
Oh, this one has no time for your embarrassing brand of radical pacifism.
Unlike you, he knows as well as I do about the importance of an occasional **beheading**.
Isn't that right, firstborn son of the House of Ghüs?
...
Seriously, did Upsher tell you how many chances I gave his meddlesome ass to get out of this alive? How I risked my goddamn neck to spare his?
All he had to do was quit chasing one lousy story -- a story he ended up bailing on anyway -- and his lover boy would still be here.
So spare me the self-righteous monologuing.
You have just as much blood on your hands as the rest of us.

You're wrong.
And you're delusional.
Our "culture" isn't addicted to violence any more than it's addicted to **shitting**.
Killing is just nature's way of expelling useless waste.
Some toxins were never meant to be absorbed into the system...
SVAPP
...and they need to get flushed the fuck out.

NO!
ZUPP
KRACK

Gale...
Stop.
I can't tell you how sick I am of people's pathetic last words.
Just shut up.
hkk
Shut up.
Shut up.
Shut --
THWOK

You boys okay?

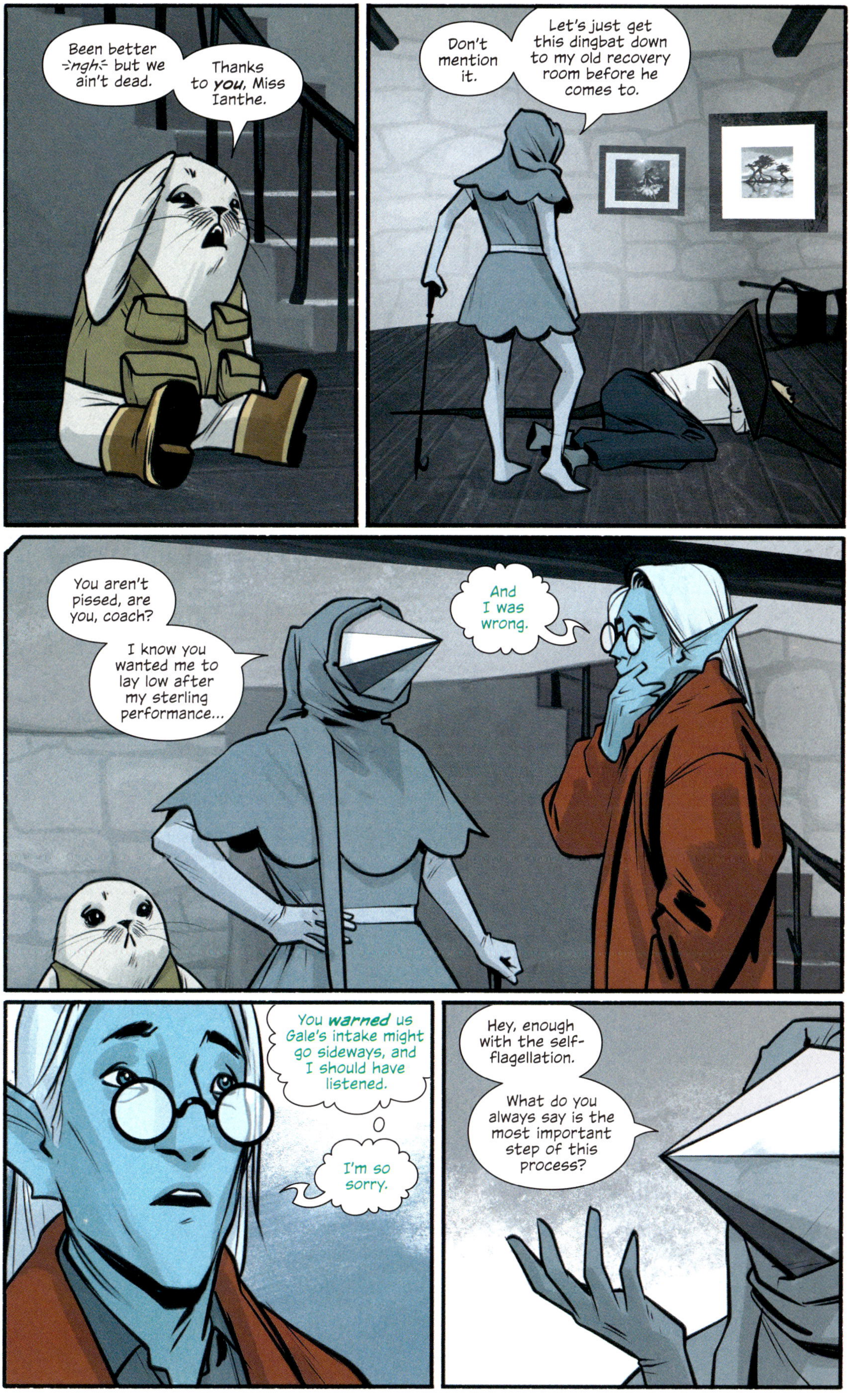
Been better =ngh= but we ain't dead.
Thanks to *you*, Miss Ianthe.
Don't mention it.
Let's just get this dingbat down to my old recovery room before he comes to.
You aren't pissed, are you, coach?
I know you wanted me to lay low after my sterling performance...
And I was wrong.
You *warned* us Gale's intake might go sideways, and I should have listened.
I'm so sorry.
Hey, enough with the self-flagellation.
What do you always say is the most important step of this process?

Forgiveness.

to be continued

Recently unearthed by co-creator Fiona Staples, presented here is a page from one of her old sketchbooks (torn out so her eldest could draw in the rest of it) featuring the very first images ever drawn of The Will, Lying Cat and Special Agent Gale.

Saga
Saga
GUNPOW
Vincent Cassel
Ed Harris
Jay Tavare

BRIAN K. VAUGHAN FIONA STAPLES
Saga

The NSFW new graphic novel from *Pride of Baghdad* creators
BRIAN K. VAUGHAN & NIKO HENRICHON
BRIAN K. VAUGHAN
NIKO HENRICHON
Spectators™
FREE to read exclusively at
ExplodingGiraffe.substack.com
SPECTATORS is ™ & © Brian K. Vaughan & Niko Henrichon. All rights reserved.